The Courier

Somebody is screwing you, Val.'

Val sat quietly, the video editor's phone call still ringing in his ears. He had received the latest shipment early this morning, already divided into envelopes. Mary had had her delivery first thing. He'd have heard long before now if there was any problem.

But he'd only checked two envelopes from the whole shipment, at random. It had become his established practice. Everything had been fine for weeks. No one would risk doctoring *half* a shipment – surely?

He sighed and climbed to his feet, staring out across the city. The stuff had only been out of his hands once since it had arrived. When the courier had picked it up from here ... If the little sod was working a fast one he'd be a cripple by teatime.

GERALD COLE

From the original screenplay by Frank Deasy

The Courier

A Thames Methuen Paperback

THE COURIER

First published in Great Britain 1988
by Methuen London Ltd
11 New Fetter Lane, London EC4P 4EE
in association with
Thames Television International Ltd
149 Tottenham Court Road, London W1P 9LL

Photosetting by Quorn Selective Repro Ltd,
Leicestershire
Printed and bound in Great Britain
by Richard Clay Ltd, Bungay, Suffolk

British Library Cataloguing in Publication Data

Cole, Gerald
  The courier.
  I. Title
  813′ 54[F]

  ISBN 0-423-02310-1

Chapter 1

Fifteen years before, the Kincora estate had been the pride of the Dublin Corporation's rehousing programme, sweeping clean the ancient, infamous slums north of the Liffey. Eight and fifteen storeys high, the residential towers rose from neat, geometrically patterned lawns. The apartments were small but well-planned, the lifts clean and properly maintained; broad picture windows gave uninterrupted views all the way to the Wicklow Mountains.

But then recession had arrived, just in time to check the finishing touches – the pubs, the community centres, the adequate bus services – which would have turned mere architecture into community. Slow decay and sporadic violence had filled the vacuum. Now the lifts no longer functioned, graffiti scarred the walls, and teenaged gangs roamed the stairwells after dark, eager for the thrills of chemistry or violence.

Gazing across the estate from a first-floor window, Val Bourke thought, *Three steps forward, two and a half back.* But that half step had given him the edge his parents, and numberless antecedents, had never known – more than enough for a man like Valentine Bourke.

A corporation refuse truck nosed into view round the corner of the adjacent tower block. As Val watched, it began to reverse laboriously, grumbling across the tarmac towards a cluster of giant bins beneath his window.

'Magic, isn't it?' spoke a voice at his back.

With an explosive hiss of air brakes, the refuse trunk thumped to a halt directly below. Blue-suited bin men

1

dropped from the cab. Val drained his tea cup and turned from the window. He was a solid man in his late thirties, his face heavy and handsome, his nose a predatory beak. He moved with an easy authority, born less of the immaculate cut of the suit he wore than the dark energy that simmered in his eyes, barely suppressed. Someone had once compared him to a priest. He liked that. The certainty, the implicit sense of order, the power. He forgot the same man had added that Val was never more dangerous than when most solicitous.

'It better be magic,' he muttered thickly.

Unease flickered in the gaze of the speaker, a thick-set, open-faced man, two years Val's junior. But only for an instant. Christy's unshaven visage shone. He was fully alive this early morning, sparkling with all the fire Val kept hidden. He was about to do what he did best.

He glanced away, grinning at a taller, younger companion, who stood tensely to one side. Both began shrugging on loose blue overalls, identical to those of the bin men below, while Val crossed the room, easing himself on to a cheap, gaudily covered sofa against the further wall.

He smiled at the young woman who sat there, pale, red-eyed, stolidly pregnant. 'You're keeping the place nice, Mary.'

The girl nodded, barely glancing his way. She seemed strung between extreme nervousness and a desperate, unspoken need, not daring to give way to either.

'How's the little fellow?'

'He's inside. Getting ready for school.'

Val nodded. 'That's great. I'll take him over in a few minutes. I'll be his uncle.'

Across the room Christy said, 'More like his Godfather.' Chuckling, he picked up a light raincoat from a low table and pulled it on. His companion bent to lift a second coat. Beneath it were disclosed two balaclava masks, a jemmy

2

and the black stubby shape of a sawn-off shotgun.

Ignoring the interruption, Val leaned closer to the girl, sliding an arm along the sofa back behind her. 'How are you, yourself, Mary?'

She shrugged minimally. 'I'm alright.'

'Are you sure?'

She blinked at him, nodding. 'Yeah.'

'Are you looking after yourself?' Val's voice was soft, low, his gaze probing her, unsettling her.

'Yeah,' she whispered.

Val nodded, dropping a hand into his jacket pocket. It emerged with a small, plastic packet of grey-white powder. He passed it to the girl, smiling in an avuncular manner as he saw her take a ragged, relieved breath, her nail-bitten fingers clutching at the transparent plastic. 'Thanks Val.'

His smile broadened at her gratitude.

'You have to be careful,' he purred. 'Promise me that, will you?'

She nodded, swallowing. 'Yeah.'

He was a bastard, she saw that. She was the best dealer on the estate, and she made him a fortune, but he always made her wait, always exacted his pound of flesh, because he knew her need was the greatest. And the worst of it was she didn't mind.

'Good girl.' His hand closed over her bony knee, squeezing it lightly. Then he rose, nodding at the two other men who stood waiting.

'OK, Sarge!' Christy snapped off a mock salute, jemmy against his shoulder.

Val laughed. Christy could always make him do that. Right back to their days in Henrietta Street when they'd been joy-riding fourteen-year-olds, getting smashed on cheap cider, dreaming of crimes that would make them famous. In his brave new world of high rise offices, burgeoning businesses, brand new BMWs, Val liked to

3

think Christy kept his feet on the ground.

The laughter was not shared with the third man. He sucked in breath as Val turned to him. 'What about you, Danny? Are you OK?'

'Yeah.' The young man's eyes, slitted and tired, shifted under Val's questioning stare. He had a gaunt, strung-out look, the look of a man on a precipice.

Bloody junkies, Val thought. *You can't trust the buggers.* He'd have to rely on Christy.

There shouldn't be any problems. A nice, neat, city centre raid. No alarm to the Garda, because the shop's system was being updated – two new young assistants who'd wet their knickers if they did anything at all. Straight in, grab the stuff and straight out. Ninety seconds at the most. And he'd pass the jewellery on personally less than twenty minutes later, in exchange for four kilos of the sweetest, purest H he'd seen on these streets in years. With that quality, and quantity, he could wrap up this whole side of the city. Everyone would have to come to him, pay his price. Sweet – very sweet, indeed.

'Good,' he murmured silkily, and smiled. 'Good.'

He turned back to the window. Behind him Christy's enthusiasm erupted into song. He growled out the theme from *Batman*: 'D'na d'na, d'na d'na – *blagman!*' And roared with full-throated laughter.

Chapter 2

Cowboys, thought Carol. *All couriers are bloody cowboys in black leather. Or cowgirls.*

She cast a disparaging look across her desk at Sharon, a pretty, round-faced blonde girl, dandling a wide-eyed, nine-month-old baby on her leathered knee. Behind her, through an open window, the rumble of the Dublin rush hour filtered up from Matt Talbot Bridge. The noise mingled with the ever-present crackle of radiophone static, the soft blare of a transistor.

'Who's collecting the baby?' Carol asked. She was a heavy, dark-haired young woman whose natural severity of feature had not been improved by the strain of managing D-Day Couriers.

'My sister,' said Sharon easily, smiling at Carol's unsuppressed sigh.

Hadn't their agreement been that the kiddy should never interfere with Sharon's work? Val Bourke expected this place to be run as a business, not a kindergarten. Carol was determined to show him just how businesslike she could be. 'When she turns up,' she said tartly, and pushed a package across the desk, 'get that over to Cabra.'

Sharon nodded, took the package and went back to her cooing.

The office door opened and a heavy-booted biker tramped across lino'd floor, as the tannoy barked on Carol's desk. Speaking into her microphone, she watched the newcomer sign in, pick up a package and exit with a wave. There was only one signature missing from the day's duty sheet. Her eyes rose to the wall clock opposite her. Five past nine.

She thumbed the microphone button. 'Three-two-four, Mark. Three-two-four, Mark. Come in please.'

Static hissed from the tannoy. Carol sighed. The guy flew like the wind when the mood was on him; she could do with a dozen like him. But every now and then he'd go blank on her, and need a stick of dynamite up his arse. *Cowboys* ...

'Three-two-four, Mark!'

'Carol?' His voice crackled from the speaker. Why was his signal breaking up? Because of intervening buildings, or was the lazy bastard still home in Marino? 'I'm stuck in Harcourt Street.'

'Good!' Carol snapped. 'Then you can collect a package from Number 30.' She caught Sharon's sympathetic glance. The fellow had the looks to charm birds from the trees – Carol had seen more than one female go cuckoo over him – but mere looks had never appealed to her. She preferred a man with more substance, more fire. Like Val Bourke, for instance. 'It's for the National General Bank,' she went on. 'Dame Street.'

There was another hiss of static.

'My angel,' purred Mark's voice.

Across the desk Sharon stifled a giggle. She knew Carol's opinion of Mark. Her eyes dropped under Carol's sudden glare.

Mark put down his radiophone on the pillow at his side and drained the last of his coffee mug.

He had woken late, surprised by and grateful for a night of dreamless sleep. The morning had been quiet, the bedroom brimming with soft light. Not so many months ago the silence of the house could still have rattled him. It was four years now – almost to the day – since his father's slow death had bequeathed him this morning silence. Time

6

enough to adjust, time enough to learn that courage needn't lie at the point of a needle.

One day at a time. That had been the rule. Building walls of selfhood, brick upon brick, testing each level for strength. Only rarely now did the foundations rock and remind him how illusory, how frail they truly were, how close the chaos beneath. For a young man of twenty-one it had been an early and a hard lesson.

He swung out of bed, slipping his feet into high, unstrapped motorcycle boots. Standing, he patted the new black leather suit that hung from the bedroom door, recent product of six months' hard-earned bonuses. Not bad for an ex-junkie. He scooped an older, scuffed jacket from the end of the bed and, shrugging it on, went downstairs.

Ten minutes down the North Strand Road. Grattan Bridge might be clear by now. He'd do it in good time.

Christy turned off Dame Street, easing the stolen Sierra through the morning traffic with inconspicuous haste. He had been a driver many times in his long and active career, and he was not about to ruin a well-wrought plan by drawing attention to himself. He was not so sure about his silent companion.

Danny was Christy's own recruit. He'd seemed eager enough at first, and he knew how to handle a sawn-off shotgun. But Christy hadn't realised how bad the fellow's habit was until today. Danny had needed a fix in Mary's toilet the moment they'd arrived; Christy had thanked his lucky stars Val hadn't been there to see it. Jesus, the fellow had taken half a syringe full, and he was still shaking like a leaf!

Christy would have to burst on to the place like a bomb. Speed and shock were the keys to this one. He couldn't leave a trembling bastard like Danny with his finger on the trigger an instant too long.

Mark made the journey in twelve minutes, bumping only two pavements, and was rewarded with the sight of a solid jam sealing Harcourt Street from side to side. With any luck another D-Day rider would have seen it too, and confirmed his alibi. Anything to keep that officious cow in the office off his back. Things had been so much easier with the previous owners.

He propped his Suzuki trailbike against a wall and stomped straight into Number 30, not even pausing to lift his visor. The office inside was large and open-plan. A receptionist looked up, startled by the loud rasp of radiophone static.

'D-Day Couriers,' Mark said.

The woman's face lightened and she picked up a package from a wire basket. As he took it, her gaze focussed on the clear blue eyes that showed through his helmet visor. 'Didn't you use to be with Speed Couriers? What happened to them?'

Mark shrugged. 'Went out of business.'

In a single weekend. One Friday, loud, foul-mouthed, overworked Frank Mehan – an ex-courier himself – had been sitting behind the microphone; the following Monday Carol was there, with a new name on the door. There'd been rumours of big money offered to the old man. Take it or leave it ultimatums. Only Carol knew the truth, and she wasn't talking. The new management was invisible.

Mark tucked the package behind his D-Day Couriers vest, and turned for the door. Outside the traffic was beginning to clear. *Magic*, he thought.

The jewellery shop was one of a row of discreetly expensive establishments off fashionable Grafton Street, all plate glass, deep-pile carpets and soft spotlighting. A clear space one shop up for the car, so no one inside would spot the number plate when they left. A quiet street. Nobody in the shop. Christy was pleased. It was looking good.

They ducked their heads below the dashboard to slip on their balaclavas. Christy held his in place with industrial goggles – there'd be glass flying about. He grinned at Danny, his mouth rendered clown-like by the shape of the mask, his eyes gleaming. 'Let's get busy, shall we?'

They cracked open the car doors, dodged across the pavement, and went in at a run.

Chapter 3

The parking space was too small for the Rover, but the tweedy, middle-aged lady behind the wheel wasn't giving up without a fight. At the fourth attempt her approach seemed perfect – just as a light-blue motorcycle zipped in behind her. Propping his bike, Mark caught sight of the woman's contorted face, mouthing imprecations over the driver's seat. Pulling off his helmet, he smiled sweetly. She roared away, crashing the gears.

He strode across the broad pavement and into the bank entrance between tall, eighteenth-century columns. The interior was large, panelled with dark wood, softly carpeted. Typewriters thudded mutedly behind a long, polished wood counter. It was minutes after opening, and the place was without customers. Only one teller stood in attendance.

'Package for the manager,' Mark announced to her, slapping it on the counter. She nodded, and moved away between the desks.

Mark drummed his fingers on the brown paper of the package, letting his gaze wander over the typists. A strawberry blonde at the far end of the counter glanced up from her work and caught his look. She blossomed suddenly with a shy, knowing smile.

Screaming, Christy burst through the shop entrance like a masked whirlwind. As the two shop assistants looked up in astonishment, he brought his jemmy smashing down on a brightly lit display counter. Three more cabinets went in a splintering hail of fragmented glass.

The young women were cowering against the wall, shocked and white, as he rounded on them, eyes blazing behind his goggles.

'He's *mental*!' he bellowed, stabbing a finger at Danny who had positioned himself in the centre of the shop. 'He'll blow your brains out!'

The girls' eyes swivelled, widening in horror as Danny trained his shotgun on them.

'Get on the floor! On the floor!' Christy screamed abruptly.

Terrified, the women huddled below the end of the counter. Christy glanced quickly at Danny, the manic gleam in his eyes instantly transformed into amused excitement. *There*, his look seemed to say, *easy as pie*.

Then he was whirling again, smashing display case after display case, raking out the contents into a canvas bag he yanked from his coat. A tray of rings spun across the shop, scattering at Danny's feet.

Turning, Danny saw Christy's back to him. He dropped quickly, snatched up one of the largest, and rose again, stuffing it into his raincoat pocket. He met the eyes of one of the assistants. 'Keep your head *down*!' he yelled. The girl jumped visibly, covering her head.

Christy ducked past him. 'The safe key!' He snapped his fingers at the assistants. 'Give!'

The girl who had seen Danny shook her head, dumb with fear. Her companion blinked at Christy, whispered, 'We don't have it. They don't keep it here . . . .'

'Come *on*!' Danny glanced edgily at the street, hands working on the shotgun stock.

Christy's eyes blazed again. 'You see!' he boomed. 'He's cracking up! He'll *shoot* you!'

Deathly pale, the girl fumbled beneath her seat, pulled out a narrow brass key and held it up. Christy snatched it

12

away.

'I didn't touch you, right?' he snapped. Pushing past her, he dropped to a small wall-safe behind the counter. He began emptying it.

'Speed!' Danny urged.

Christy glanced up at the girls and smiled. 'Fellow's got drugs on the brain,' he said affably.

The whiteness of the girl's dress caught Mark's eye first. It was a long shift, flowing but carefully tailored to show off the slim, lithe figure of its owner. Not that it needed showing off. As she paused beside the furthest desk, bending to answer a query, he saw her face, and his heart thudded. Surely not?

It had been over three years since he'd last seen those features – dead white, then, under thick make-up, and black-dyed, punkishly spiked hair. Now the make-up was barely visible, the hair its natural auburn, shaped to the base of a slender neck. It was a beautiful face, oval, full-lipped, dark-eyed. Could a schoolboy crush last nearly four years?

He couldn't help his wondering, excited grin. 'Colette!' he called.

She looked up, and blinked in surprised recognition. Then she was moving towards him, lips curving in a warm, astonished smile. 'Mark? I haven't seen you in years.'

He laughed, delighted. 'You look great.'

'So do you.'

She stood on the further side of the counter, drinking him in. She looked stunning, so *businesslike*; if she hadn't been smiling she'd have scared the pants off him.

'I thought you'd left,' he said. 'Gone away.'

'No.' She grinned. 'Still here.'

Christ, he was going scarlet. How many times had he dreamed of a conversation like this?

13

'We're getting old,' he said.

Her eyebrows lifted. 'Speak for yourself.'

They laughed, leaving a smiling silence where both seemed suddenly vulnerable.

'Look at you,' Mark said quickly. 'Working in a bank.'

'Yeah.' She nodded, admitting the incongruity of it. Her punk days were long gone.

'You're not the manager, are you?'

'In this place?' She chuckled. 'You must be joking.' Her smile softened. 'How are you really, Mark?'

He paused, realising he'd abstracted only the best part of a past that now seemed dark, confused, guilt-ridden – a past he'd rather keep private. 'I'm fine,' he said.

'You're sure?' Her concern surprised, and touched him.

'I'm great,' he smiled.

Reassured, she let her own smile broaden, become coquettish. 'We ought to have a drink some evening.'

Mark's heart bumped again. Not a snatched lunchtime for old times' sake – the chance of a whole *evening*.

'What time do you knock off at?' he said quickly.

'Today?' She laughed, surprised, but not displeased. 'Three o'clock.'

'I'll pick you up.' He was already backing away from the counter, not risking her second thoughts.

'Hold on a sec,' she said quickly. 'I'm meeting Danny. Can you make it four?'

Mark's face dropped fractionally, the name hanging between them. Then he shrugged it off. 'Sure. Four o'clock.'

Colette's grin was spreading. She nodded at the package still grasped in his hand. 'Mark, I think I take that.'

He raised his eyebrows, and handed it over. 'Getting a bit forgetful.'

'Don't forget four o'clock.' Her smile was slyly affectionate, a sweet feline promise.

'I won't,' he murmured. 'See you.'

He left the building on a cushion of air, doubting the reality of the day.

Sweet Jesus, Colette Adams. A girl he'd ached for at the age of seventeen, a girl he'd seen whisked away on the bikes and battered passenger seats of fellows in their twenties and even thirties. What chance would a spotty teenager have stood with a lively, confident desperately attractive nineteen-year-old? Until now. It was like the start of every wicked dream of his adolescence. He really must be growing up at last.

And the only shadow that remained was cast by her brother Danny. Danny, the big man who'd first turned him on to smack, Danny, the best friend he'd abandoned to the world of H because he saw both their lives trickling away through the point of a hypodermic. . . . But that was a darkness he couldn't face yet. One brick at a time. Stick to the rules. And this was the most promising brick he'd been handed in a long, long time.

Chapter 4

The Sierra bumped a Kincora kerb and skidded to a halt in the shadow of a tower block. Laughing, mask-less now, Christy leapt from the car, canvas bag clasped in his hand.

No less nervous than before, Danny joined him, glancing round quickly at the desolate acres as they ran towards the block entrance. Through a swing door, past a doorway, into a dank stairwell, smelling of garbage and urine.

Panting, they paused to throw off their raincoats. Christy tossed his canvas bag behind a bulging refuse sack. Then they were running again – down an ill-lit corridor, through a further door flanked by giant metal bins.

The back of the corporation refuse trunk faced them, the engine ticking over. Blue-uniformed now, both men sprang on to the rear platform, thumping the vehicle's side. 'Go!' Danny yelled. 'Fuck it – go!' The truck lurched away across the estate.

Footsteps echoed in the tower block stairwell, one set slow and steady, the other neat and fast. Smiling, Val descended into the light of the entrance hall, holding the hand of a small boy of about seven with a school satchel hanging from his shoulder.

'Wait there a minute, Michael,' he said as they reached the bottom of the stairs. Ducking to one side, he fumbled behind a refuse sack and retrieved the bag Christy had dropped.

'Here it is,' he smiled at the boy. 'I thought I dropped it around here somewhere.' He squatted down beside the child, his face looming close. 'Will you do me a favour,

Michael? I've nowhere to put my things until I reach my car. Can I slip it in your bag?'

Eagerly the boy jerked the satchel off his shoulder and held it open. Val popped the bag into the musty interior, next to sandwiches wrapped clumsily in plastic and rubber bands.

'Good boy.' Smiling, Val rose.

Yes, a nice, neat, morning's work, with a good weight to the proceeds. And no one to see a thing that might connect him with the incident – only a well-known local businessman helping out a friend on the estate. Every day should be as good.

He took the boy's hand again and went out into the daylight.

'What's a blagman, Val?' the boy asked, looking up at him.

'A blagman?' Val considered. Then he grinned. 'He's like Batman, Michael. Batman and Robin. A sort of a hero. . . .'

Danny peered at himself in the hairdresser's mirror, turning his head from side to side. The newly dyed blond of his hair only seemed to emphasise the pallor of his flesh. But he'd been feeling sick since first thing this morning – sick from fear. And now the fear was a habit, grinding at his nerves.

Leaning across from the next chair, Christy, his stubble gone, his hair slick from shampoo, tapped Danny's arm, startling him. 'It's consciousness,' Christy snapped. 'Total consciousness. You know what I mean, don't you, Alfie?'

Christy's cutter – a lean, life-marked man staving off his forties with baggy pants and a leopardskin tee-shirt – nodded approvingly.

Christy's eyes were sparkling, the adrenalin of the raid still rife in his veins. 'You go in with your shooter, right? And your mind's expanded – you've got four eyes and four ears, totally alert. Zap! Split-second decisions.' He grinned

18

wolfishly, relishing the memory. 'It's beautiful.' His voice becames a caress. 'It's like a woman – like a hundred women.' Then he shook his head in contemptuous disapproval. 'Much better than that crap you jack into yourself. Robbers always live well. Junkies? Junkies live like shit.'

He twisted round abruptly. 'You see that, don't you, Alfie?' Behind him Alfie grunted agreement, and made another attempt to steady Christy's bobbing head.

'I even told my daughter,' Christy went on. 'A robber'll put a house around you. A junkie? He'll sell every stick of furniture you own.' He gazed at Danny, his look growing softer, almost paternal. 'You should do more stroking, Danny – I'm telling you – cut this stuff out.'

Danny nodded faintly, his face strained, enduring the lecture. He wanted to be gone.

With a resigned sigh, Christy reached under his sheet and pulled out a small packet of white powder. He smiled mirthlessly. 'Here's your prezzie from Uncle Val.' He glanced up at Alfie's reflection. 'Uncle Val the junkies' pal!' They both laughed.

Danny snatched the packet and stood up. 'Ta, Christy.'

As he stuffed it into his trouser pocket, Christy nodded to it. 'You've a good month there, Danny. Think about it – hitting banks – it's got to be better.'

'Yeah, maybe.' Danny was already moving towards the street door. 'Different strokes, Christy.'

'See you, Danny.' Christy swivelled in his chair to watch him go. 'Oh and hey, hey, hey!' His accent became instantly transatlantic. 'Be careful out there!'

Danny grunted, and patted his trouser pocket. 'I won't *be* out there,' he said.

Chapter 5

Detective Inspector John Patrick McGuigan was not, technically speaking, a true Dubliner. He had been born to the west of the city, in County Kildare, the son of a farmer who'd been the son of a farmer before him. When the farm had failed (a tale so tragic it was repeated endlessly in family circles), the McGuigans had trekked east to the banks of the Liffey. It had taken him ten years, McGuigan was wont to tell anyone who would listen, to shake the sods from his shoes.

But, in its insidious and charming way, the city had claimed him. He had warmed to the fading grandeur of its architecture, the intimacy of its pubs. It had been a provincial city then, in the forties, a countryman's idea of a metropolis. Its earthiness and its quick intelligence had appealed to the young McGuigan. He was intelligent himself, within the bounds of a strict morality drummed into him by the priests. The human heart held a particular fascination for him. He believed in Good and Evil as absolutes.

His family had not approved when he had applied to join the Garda. There had never been a policeman in the family before. They were law-abiding, for the most part, but they preferred to keep the law at a polite distance.

But McGuigan had prospered. Moving steadily through the ranks, he had watched the city boom, outpacing itself in its bid to catch up with the twentieth century. Neon signs along stately O'Connell Street; higgledy-piggledy housing developments thrown up on the outskirts. Incongruous growths of modernity, and each new one bringing another, more exotic crime – revealing a fresh, an uglier aspect of the human heart.

Were things really so much worse or, after thirty years in the force, was he finally succumbing to the laments of middle age? Sitting in his car opposite Kincora shopping centre, watching the brave new world pass by, McGuigan refused to commit himself. All he knew was that the countryman's Dublin had gone, and in its place flourished excrescences like Valentine Bourke.

He nodded at a shop front along the parade, a bright red and yellow sign in illuminated plastic, VAL'S FOR VALUE. 'Look at our Valentine now. Don't we all know that "every intelligent man dreams of being a gangster"?'

The broad, hard-faced young man at his side frowned at him in confusion. 'You think these people are intelligent?'

'Course they are,' McGuigan said. 'But the same author says, "Power settles everything".'

Christ, thought Detective Sergeant Dunne, *the old fellow's off again.*

McGuigan smiled the Cheshire cat smile that had chilled a thousand suspects with its incongruous warmth. 'It's all a question of power,' he explained.

Dunne grunted non-committally. Old John Patrick might have been a wizard in his time, but his blarney meant bugger all today. They knew who the bastards were, they knew how they operated – why didn't they just wade in and crack heads?

Still smiling, McGuigan opened the car door. It was hardly fair to quote Camus to a junior officer who had trouble spelling Dun Laoghaire, but there had to be some privileges left for age and experience.

'Let's talk to the man,' he said.

The youth had the frame of a featherweight, a stunted,

muscular body under an old man's head. He had clearly steeled himself for this approach.

'Listen, Val, can I make a deal with you?'

Val glanced up from the stack of fluffy Taiwanese toys that he was price-marking. Ranks of similar items, all gaudily coloured and cheap, filled the shelves at his back. He knew the kid, a new user from Belclare Avenue, up by the park. Mary should have been taking care of him. Val never dealt direct. The kid should know that.

'No.' Val shook his head. He resumed price-marking. 'I don't know what you're talking about, Joe.'

The youth twitched, his dark, button eyes darting about the shop. The only other occupant was an assistant, stacking goods at the far end of the counter, carefully ignoring the conversation.

'I've got two Visa cards,' the youth hissed, reaching into the back pocket of his jeans.

'No.' Val didn't raise his head. 'I don't want to know.'

The shop door swung open.

Looking up now, Val broke into a broad smile. 'Hello, Mr McGuigan!' he called.

Panic reared in the youth's eyes; he froze.

Quashing his unease, Val watched the policeman amble inside, his henchman hanging back by the door. McGuigan's long, lantern-jawed face bore his self-satisfied cat look – a look Val knew of old. What in God's name was the old bastard doing here this morning? It was less than an hour after the raid. Christ, he'd only just unloaded the take.

'Still in business, Val?'

McGuigan halted behind the paralysed youth, as Val shrugged easily. 'Just about. You know how it is.'

McGuigan nodded, his gaze roving across the rows of toys to the newspapers and magazines displayed on the shop counter. It came to rest on the young man standing immobile in front of him.

'Taking a lot of interest in the local youth lately, Val,' he smiled. 'Taking kids to school?'

The colour drained from Val's cheeks. His eyes hardened.

'I *care* about those kids, McGuigan.' He gestured angrily with the price-marker. 'You may not believe this, but ask anyone around here – they'll tell you. Ask the teachers!'

McGuigan's smile tightened. Val the spider, Val the evil hub of a grubby manipulative web whose existence everyone denied, because informers got their kneecaps shattered, their faces removed by shotgun blast, or worse. He couldn't touch him – yet – but he could rattle him.

'Little boys now, is it, Val?'

Unnoticed, disbelieving his luck, the youth was backing towards the door. Dunne snatched him from behind, slammed him bodily against the shop window.

'You watch that glass!' Val roared.

Reaching down, McGuigan reversed a tabloid so that Val could see the headline. CHILD SEX FIEND ON THE RUN, it announced, beside a picture of a smiling, lingerie-clad model. 'People don't like it,' he said coldly.

Val's lip curled in contempt. 'People don't like *filth*, McGuigan.' *He's got nothing*, the thought dinned through his brain. *It's a try on. He's pissing in the wind.*

'Oh you're a wit.' McGuigan's look was glacial. He was seeing something that had crawled from a charnel house, something whose very existence offended him deeply and personally.

He moved to the door, where Dunne was grilling the youth. 'Let him go,' he said, and turned to Val, spitting out the words, 'Let the fish swim.'

Bastard! Val watched the policemen go, his face working, his heart thudding. No one spoke to him like that to his face – no one!

He breathed in, forcing the rage to settle, knowing it

24

would do him no good. Then he moved down the counter, slapping the price-marker into his assistant's hand. 'Get that stuff sorted out,' he said.

'But the stacking?'

'Don't.' Val raised a hand, eyes closed. 'Just do it.' He moved on into the back of the shop.

Someone was talking on the estate. Someone was whispering to the filth. He had to speak to Christy.

Chapter 6

There was a niggling problem with a reconciliation and Colette did not get away from the bank until almost three thirty. Hurrying to the café where they'd arranged to meet, she found Danny crouched over two emptied cups.

She surprised him with a swift peck on the cheek, whispered an apology, added quickly, 'I'm starving!' and moved straight to the self-service counter. She wasn't hungry, of course, having had a perfectly adequate lunch, but the habit of succouring her younger brother was well-established with both of them.

She gave him a warm grin as she returned, her tray heaped with two more coffees, sandwiches and biscuits. As he thanked her, she noticed his hair and chuckled. 'You're looking very cool.'

He ducked away self-consciously as she ruffled his fringe.

'No, it's nice,' she insisted, sitting. 'I like it, anyway.'

She handed him a cup, watching his grin fade behind the lines of strain. The closeness of their childhood and teens had lessened now, weakened by a short-lived flight Danny had made to England eighteen months before. But they still met two or three times a month. She still worried about him.

'So how are the folks?' he asked.

'They're OK.' Colette paused, not wishing to suggest blame. 'They'd like to see you.'

Danny grunted, hiding his face in the coffee cup. Then his smile resurfaced. He reached into his jacket pocket. 'I got you a present.'

Colette looked at him in astonishment. 'What for?' Getting him to acknowledge that she *had* a birthday was a family joke.

Grinning, he held out a gold ring with a huge, glittering diamond. Colette took it, stared open-mouthed, then burst into laughter. 'We're not getting engaged!'

Danny's face instantly dropped.

'Oh come on, Daniel,' Colette chided, refusing to let him feel hurt. 'It *is* funny.'

His face set, he turned away. Colette looked at the ring more closely, saw the size and value of the diamond. Her smile died. It had to be worth hundreds; she knew Danny wasn't working.

'It's hot, isn't it?' she said flatly. 'You're using again.'

Danny rounded on her, his look suddenly vicious. 'Do I ask you what you're doing? Do I ask you who you're *screwing*?'

Colette blinked, shocked and hurt by his vehemence, but even more by the knowledge that it confirmed her suspicion. He had gone to London to break the habit; she had given him the fare; she had thought all that was behind him now.

He was silent, not daring to look at her, locked in his own misery.

'What's happening to you?' she said.

He shook his head. 'I don't know.'

Feeling his pain, she reached her hand across to his. 'Try a programme. Try something.' She paused. 'I met Mark today.'

Interest sparked in Danny's eyes. As he looked up, Colette said, 'He was asking for you.'

'Yeah? How is he?'

Colette smiled. 'He looks great. He …'

'Still into the bikes?' Danny's face hardened into a look very close to contempt.

28

Colette frowned. Danny and Mark had been inseparable. She knew they'd both been using, but then Mark had stopped. Was that any reason for Danny to show this – hatred? He was her brother, and she just couldn't understand him any more.

'He's OK, Danny. He is – really.'

Things were happening between her and Mark. She could not bear it if finding Mark meant that she lost Danny.

Danny picked up one of the biscuits on his sister's plate. Saying nothing, he began to chew.

Mark was back home by a quarter to four, having pleaded bike problems to a frankly disbelieving Carol. He didn't care – seeing Colette was a damn sight more important than D-Day Couriers.

He was brushing his teeth when she called. She'd been delayed with Danny, and she still had to change. Could he pick her up from home? She was still with her parents in Clontarf.

No problem. He'd ride to Cork to see her if he had to, and he could hear it in his voice as he spoke. With any other girl he'd have stifled that eagerness, feeling stupid. With Colette it didn't seem to matter.

Washed, dressed in clean shirt and jeans, he checked the bedroom, shaking the duvet into place. He didn't want to think about sex. Making plans, he sensed, could ruin everything. He'd simply go with whatever happened, or did not. But there was no point in being unprepared.

Helmetless, shrieking, Colette clung to Mark's waist as the trailbike bumped on to the broad expanse of Dollymount beach, then struck out across the level, hard-packed sand, accelerating as it went. To the right spread the grey, level sea, overshadowed by docks and derricks and cut by the long black line of the Bull Wall. Ahead stretched three miles of unblemished strand, rising into heaped and tussocked dunes.

There was a chill to the afternoon and the sky was dull, but the sea air ruffling Colette's hair and squeezing under her sunglasses blew away more than the day's cobwebs. She could not remember when she had felt so exhilarated – by the reckless speed of the bike, by Mark's close physical presence. It seemed years since she had experienced a physical reaction to anyone.

A mile down the beach, Mark swerved suddenly to the left, switchbacking upwards into the dunes. He laughed as Colette shrieked again, thumping his back in protest as the bike slewed under them. 'Stop! Mark, *stop*!'

He jolted to a halt. Giving out a loud whoop, he flung himself down against a low dune, chuckling back at Colette as she took the handlebars. Her face was flushed and grinning.

'Is this what I got dressed up for?' she accused.

He chuckled louder and plucked at a clump of dune grass. 'Do you want to go for a drink?'

'Yeah.' She cocked her head, her grin broadening. 'We'll go into Duggan's Hotel.'

He laughed. 'You must be joking!'

'No.' Her grin was unchanged.

'Duggan's – Jesus.' Mark shook his head. The past really was catching up on him. 'I haven't been in there for years.'

Colette held out her hand. 'Let's see what it's like now.'

The lounge was both spacious and intimate, islands of warm light around a central, dimly lit bar. The place had had a face-lift since Mark had last seen it; the familiar tattiness replaced by discreet designer colours, the cheap porter by ambiguously titled cocktails. But the atmosphere had not changed greatly. Or perhaps it was just Colette, because they had the bar to themselves. Perched on stools, heads bowed together, they were cordially abandoned by the barman.

Mark did not notice. All he was aware of was a tingling glow that enclosed him from head to foot. It was all so easy, so right. He had never been like this with anyone before, never talked so freely.

'See that chair over there?' Colette nodded to a secluded corner. 'Johnny English felt me up on that chair.' She chuckled. '*And* I let him!'

Mark grunted. The terrible trio. Danny, Johnny and Mark. Except Johnny was a whole year older, and had the chat to go with his advanced age. 'Toy-boy Johnny,' he said.

'Danny and you were all there,' Colette reminded him.

Mark laughed. He remembered too well. 'I always wanted to take someone upstairs.'

Colette leaned closer, letting her hair brush his cheek. 'I fancied you even then.' She gave him a quick smile. 'But I thought it would have been babysnatching – being Danny's big sister.'

'Sometimes,' said Mark, 'when we'd be down in your house, supposed to be studying, I'd be in your bedroom. And I loved it. Just looking at your clothes – your make-up . . . .'

Tickled, Colette gave a chuckle, her grin broadening lecherously. 'You were wanking in my bedroom!' She wagged an accusatory finger.

'No.' Mark caught her finger. 'But I hated Johnny.'

Colette grew serious. 'Johnny wasn't that good, after all.' She turned her face up to him, fanning the hand he held so her fingertips touched his cheek. 'I should have corrupted you.'

Mark's lips moved down on to hers; her kiss felt soft and warm, creating the mildest of detonations in the back of his skull. Coming up for air, he felt his senses swim.

31

He grinned. 'You had acne.'

Colette's eyes narrowed. 'Not when you still had blackheads . . . .'

Their smiles softened into a second kiss. This time her mouth opened, and she sank into him. Mark felt a heavy, piston thump in his chest. Breathing in, he slid his hand along Colette's thigh. But she eased herself away from him, her lips brushing down his cheek to his ear.

'No,' she whispered. 'Come on upstairs . . . .'

Chapter 7

Her sweetness filled him. It wasn't just sex without false promises, or fumbled approaches or lingering guilt. It was the most sublime *fun*. As he moved in her, she moved in him. He had never thought one person could make him feel so impossibly liberated. If he'd had the energy he'd have burst into song. Instead, lying in happy exhaustion, he grinned at her as she lay across his chest, gazing into his face while her finger stroked his cheek.

'You looked really gorgeous in your fancy dress this morning,' she told him.

He winked at her. 'Fancy me, did you?'

Her smile spread. 'Why do you think you're here?' Bowing her head, she kissed him lightly. 'You look really sexy in black.'

'Yeah?'

'Yeah,' she purred, then erupted into violent squirming giggles as he brought his hands up under her arms, tickling her. 'Mark, don't! *Mark!*'

He stopped, leaving them both breathless. Quiet now, she looked down at him, her face softening.

'I really like being with you.' Her voice was almost a whisper.

Mark swallowed. 'I couldn't believe it when I saw you this morning.'

This time the kiss was deep and engaging, a pledge that absorbed them both. As they parted, both were breathing deep, their faces flushed and fragile. It was Colette who smiled first, reasserting a necessary normality.

'I want a cigarette,' she admitted.

'Go on.' He patted her rump. Grinning, she threw back the sheet. She picked her shirt up off the carpet and pulled it over her head. Mark reached across and ruffled her hair. 'What happened to the spikes?'

She laughed. 'I grew up,' she told him.

He pushed himself higher up the pillow and sat watching her as she found her cigarettes, then settled on the bedroom's broad windowsill, her head against the pale blinds, one well-shaped leg extended. She seemed to him utterly mysterious, utterly beautiful; every movement, every breath fascinated him.

She smiled at his scrutiny, then she lit a cigarette and inhaled.

'What's it like in the bank?' Mark asked.

'It's alright.' She exhaled. 'It's pretty boring. I always wanted to leave . . . .'

'Why didn't you?'

'I was going to, but then it got really bad with Danny.' She gave the faintest of shrugs. 'It wasn't on.'

'I never thought you'd stay living at home.' It didn't fit Mark's lingering image of the glamorous free spirit, the girl who lived in a world he couldn't enter. He was recasting his view of her with every passing moment.

She looked at him suddenly. 'I really envied you when your father died.' He blinked, his expression quizzical. 'You were *free*! You could have done anything. Sold the house – left . . . .'

Mark's smile was ironic. How could he tell her he had never felt more trapped, more lost at that time? He swung out of bed, joining her at the window.

'Why didn't you?' she persisted.

He shrugged. 'I don't know.'

'You still could.' She turned her head, trying to read his smile. 'Danny always said you stopped using because you wanted something better.'

This time he laughed. 'Right now I want a beer.'

'No really.' Her face was serious. 'What *do* you want?'

He looked away from her. It had been a long time since he had revealed his deepest thoughts and feelings to anyone – as long ago as Danny. There was nothing he found easy to share; no one he trusted enough to lower the self-imposed barrier.

He took a breath. 'I want,' he said, 'one part of life that's no lies, no cover-ups. That's what I want.'

Gazing at him, Colette nodded thoughtfully, and her smile slowly resurfaced. 'I see what he meant.'

Mark grinned back at her, then made her start with a gentle tickle. 'No you don't,' he assured her. They kissed.

But I do, she thought. *I do*.

Chapter 8

It was stupidity, blind, mindless stupidity. Why hadn't he gone home like he'd planned? Why hadn't he curled up with Uncle Val's prezzie? Instead he'd insisted on calling Colette, insisted on seeing her so that he could get his brain straight, touch the bed-rock again which she'd always represented. Only that had gone as sour as everything else. He couldn't reach her any more. And – the final bitterness – she was seeing that bastard, that Judas, Mark. His own bloody sister.

None of it made any sense, nothing he thought, nothing he did. He knew the wrongness was in him, but it made no difference. Whatever he did, the world twisted against him.

He was wandering down by the quays, late, near Duggan's Hotel, when the Garda car eased to a halt beside him. 'Danny Adams, is it? I hear your probation officer's missing a call from you.'

It was a young policeman he knew well. It would have been easy enough to grovel, to apologise, to go through the motions. He didn't have the heart. He kept walking.

Two of them pinned him against rough brick. One held him, the other rifled his pockets. The smack wasn't even hidden in a handkerchief. Colette's ring was next to it.

'Oh Danny,' the young policeman said, 'you're not being a naughty boy again, are you?'

Then they cautioned him and locked him up for the night. He had nine hours to ponder his stupidity.

By six the next morning his skin was crawling. There were sharp spikes behind his eyes; his stomach ached;

perspiration sheened his forehead. Sweet Jesus, nearly twenty-four hours since his last hit. He had not slept at all.

At six thirty he was delivered to an interview room, a square, windowless place without colour and bare but for a table, three plastic chairs and a large metal filing cabinet. He sat alone for twenty minutes, shivering and listening to the dull murmur of a ventilator. Then the door opened and a tall, hulking young man entered. He had lank blond hair, the face of a boxer. He introduced himself as Detective Sergeant Dunne.

Hoisting himself on to the table next to Danny, he gave a swift, mirthless smile. 'I hear you're a good friend of Christy O'Connor, Danny. You know, the guy who's terrible fond of jewellery. He's a bad man.'

Danny's heart thudded. Was this what it was really all about? He was not up to these sort of games. He breathed in. 'I'd like a drink of water.'

'Sure.' Dunne nodded reasonably. 'They tell me Christy's a good friend of Val Bourke. You'll know Val, of course.'

Danny sighed to hide a sudden shudder, his head dropping. 'I feel sick.'

'Do you now?' Dunne stood, looming over the younger man.

There was a moment's pause. Confused, Danny lifted his head. A fist drove into his chest, just below the heart. He cried out, more in shock than pain, lurching backwards in his chair. But Dunne caught him by an arm and the front of his tee-shirt, yanking him upright as the chair thumped on to its side.

'Is your memory improving, Danny? We're talking about Val Bourke – you can shout as loud as you like, because no one'll hear you down here.'

Danny stumbled back, pulling away from Dunne's grasp. Fear worked in his eyes. He couldn't cope with this.

'Are you listening, Danny?' Dunne advanced on him,

prodding his chest. 'The name is V-A-L. You rob for him. He keeps you in little goodies . . . .'

Danny retreated, shaking his head. 'I don't know him.'

'I'm not a fool, Danny. I know when someone's shooting me a line.'

'No . . . .' Danny's heel struck the front of the metal filing cabinet. Sweat poured out of him. Dunne looked like a bloody maniac.

His hands suddenly shot out, grabbed Danny by the shoulders. 'Do you want to go inside, Danny?' He jerked Danny backwards, slamming his head against the metal. 'Do you? *Do* you!'

'I don't know Val Bourke! I don't know anything about him!'

Danny's head crashed again. 'Come *on!*'

'I never heard of him!' This time he cried out as he hit the metal.

The door opened. Abruptly Dunne stood back, his hands dropping. The squat figure of McGuigan was silhouetted in the doorway. He paused, allowing the room to absorb the full impact of his appearance, then he ambled in, his long face grave and calm. He was humming quietly under his breath. 'Oh Danny boy, the pipes, the pipes are calling . . . .'

Danny watched him, relief mingled with a much greater fear. If it was McGuigan it was really serious. They weren't messing around. They had something that would stick.

Moving up close to Danny, the detective looked into the young man's face. Then, apparently satisfied, he clapped a hand on his shoulder and turned towards the table. There was no pressure in the grasp, no urgency; it was the gesture of a father, or a priest, an authority built on impersonal concern. Danny found himself obeying it without thought.

Behind them, Dunne turned and left without a word.

The two men sat down on opposite sides of the table, McGuigan depositing a thick file on the table top and leaning back in his chair; his tune faded into silence as he studied Danny.

Under the unhurried scrutiny, Danny's relief turned to unease. He began to fidget.

'I'm a bogman, Danny,' McGuigan spoke at last, his voice a soft drawl. 'I like those old songs.'

Danny sighed. He'd had the McGuigan charm before – a good four years of it, on and off. He wanted to know what the man had. But John Patrick was not to be hurried.

'Are you strung out, Dan?' McGuigan asked.

Danny looked at him. He could see no irony in the older man's eyes, no yawning pitfall. He nodded warily.

'We'll sort that out for you. We'll sort out a methadone programme.'

Danny breathed in. This was new – offered so matter-of-factly, so easily. No one was that generous.

'These charges – ' McGuigan tapped the file on the table, the gesture almost dismissive. 'I prefer to draw people out, Dan. These younger fellows – ' he nodded in the direction Dunne had gone ' – they're all out to make a mark. I prefer to draw people out .... '

He let his words hang, stirring suspicion and hope in the younger man's mind. Was he offering a deal?

'I'd like,' McGuigan resumed, 'to see Val more ...' He shrugged. 'More out in the open. That's all.' His gaze was calm and accepting. Tell me anything, it said, tell me anything, and I will absolve you.

Danny's eyes dropped to the charge file. Well-thumbed pages covering years of fifth-rate crime, petty theft, mugging, forgery, possession, possession, possession .... Yesterday morning he had known more fear than he had ever thought possible. He had entered a new league with Val. And Val controlled things now. Val was the source. There'd be no escaping him.

Sweet God, to be shot of it all! No one else had offered

even the faintest glimmer of hope. He could not live any more without hope – and damn the consequences. He made up his mind.

'It's a trade.' He spoke hesitantly. 'Val's trading the jewels for the smack.'

McGuigan frowned, not understanding. Danny leaned forward across the table, the words coming in a rush. 'Some people are into banks one day, jewels the next, smack the next. Val just wants to be into smack.'

'Everywhere?' McGuigan asked. His soporific manner had gone.

'No, just his side of town.' Danny's grunt was ironic. 'It's the coming thing.'

McGuigan nodded. He had waited a long time for this moment, longer than he cared to remember.

Chapter 9

Still wrapped in the intimacy of the night, they walked out of the hotel, giggling at the look on the receptionist's face.

'They think I'm on the game,' Colette protested.

Mark grinned at her. 'You'd make a fortune!' She cuffed him playfully, and they turned the corner on to Eden Quay.

It was a steely, unforgiving morning; the first charges of the rush hour being made across O'Connell Bridge. A silence fell between them. Feeling it, Mark said, 'Are you sure you don't want a lift to work?'

'No.' Colette shook her head. 'I like to walk.'

They had reached the parked bike. Mark swung himself on to the saddle. Colette rested her hand on the handlebars, toying with the controls. She looked at Mark, her smile suddenly fragile. 'So?' she said.

'This is more like leaving you home from a dance,' he said.

She laughed, glad of the opportunity.

'I'll ring you at home,' Mark told her.

He saw the uncertainty rise in her face and reached out a hand, covering hers. 'I will,' he promised.

They kissed, a last flurry of warmth. Then, with a hurried 'See you', she was gone in the thickening crowds.

Mark slipped on his helmet. He felt triumphant and tired, but pleasantly so. Dreams did not come true so often that he could cope easily with the result. Something momentous had entered his life, something so big he couldn't judge it yet. All he knew was that he felt good for the first time in ages.

He kick-started the Suzuki and roared off into the morning.

The girl on reception lifted her head from her magazine just high enough to read the name on the package. 'Upstairs,' she grunted. 'High as you can go.'

He tramped up the broad, uncarpeted staircase. It was a converted warehouse, the bare brick painted red, squiggles of bright neon lighting the way. The top landing was in semi-darkness.

Rock music blared from a video editing desk against a far wall. Images writhed on a bank of monitors. A young man in a tee-shirt sat at the controls, fingers flying from button to button, eyes flitting from screen to screen.

Mark approached and dropped the package at his elbow.

'Thanks a lot, man.' Fumbling across the desk, the editor snatched up a biro and scrawled a signature on the receipt pad.

Mark nodded at the monitors. 'Pop video?'

'Yeah. New U2.' The editor grinned. 'But they got chicks.'

His hand rummaged blindly under mounds of discarded plastic cups, unearthed a second package and held it over his shoulder. As Mark took it, he said, 'Keep coming, and I'll get you tickets for a gig.'

'Thanks.' Mark was pleasantly surprised, too used to the anonymity of the courier. As he turned to go, the editor asked, 'Are you into racing?'

The question caught Mark unawares.

'Yeah.'

'Cool.'

The editor's fingers danced across the controls. Since Mark's arrival his eyes had not left the monitors for a second.

Shaking his head in amusement, Mark retreated down

the stairs.

The return delivery was to a modern office block north of the city centre. He knew the building. He had called there two or three times before. Braking for the first traffic light in O'Connell Street, he heard a horn blast to his right. He turned his head and saw a D-Day courier in a red leather scrambling suit.

Sharon raised her visor and mouthed above the traffic roar: 'How many left?'

Mark lifted a single gloved finger.

The girl nodded. Mark caught the flash of a cheeky smile. 'Race you back!' she called.

Grinning, Mark raised his thumb. The lights changed.

Engine screaming, Sharon peeled off into Abbey Street. Mark wrenched on his throttle.

He was doing forty down a cobbled cut-through off Parnell Street when the red Renault jerked out of an alleyway. Braking was only a gesture. His front wheel struck a nearside tyre. He felt the handlebars wrenched from his grip, and the world up-ended. His left leg took the impact of the landing. Then he was rolling across damp cobbles, his helmet bumping on the stone. A bend in the kerb stopped him.

He lay curled up and motionless, while his thoughts re-emerged from that still centre to which they retreated at such moments of danger. When they had, he felt the ache in his leg, a dull booming in his head.

He sat up, wincing. He had been lucky to be wearing full leathers. Nothing felt broken. His D-Day Couriers vest hung from his chest, a tie-strap torn. As he pulled the vest straight a fifty-pound note dropped from inside and fluttered on to the cobbles. He blinked in disbelief. Then he lifted the vest. His delivery package fell out. It was split down the middle. A twenty-pound note was visible through the gap.

Raising his head, he saw the cobbles behind him were strewn with scraps of paper coloured brown and green and blue. Bank notes – twenties, fifties, hundreds! – littering the roadway.

Abruptly his senses sharpened; he knew he was not hallucinating. Ignoring the pain in his leg, he scrambled across the cobbles, jamming the notes back into the damaged package.

'Hey! You OK there?' A man in a cap stood by the driver's door of the Renault, looking anxious and annoyed.

'Sure,' Mark called, working faster. 'I'm fine. Never better.' His leg throbbed mercilessly.

Despite the pain, he took the stairs to the D-Day office, hanging back behind the cover of the lift to see if the coast was clear. The radio crackled through the half-open door.

Carol was not behind her desk. He breathed in, giving thanks for his luck. Then he squeezed through the door.

There was a note cellotaped to the filing cabinet behind Carol's chair. 'Been and gone! xxxx Shar.'

Snatching it down, Mark began to attack the desk drawers. Only one seemed unlocked. Opening it, he pulled out a fresh courier packet and dropped it on the desk top. Then – eyes constantly flitting to the door – he brought the damaged packet from his satchel and began stuffing bundles of notes into the new envelope.

He had just sealed it when he heard the whine of the lift. Heart thumping, he pulled a sticky label off a dispenser, slapped it on the package and hurriedly began copying the address from the torn envelope. He barely had time to push the emptied package into his satchel when Carol stepped through the door.

Her face registered surprise, and then turned instantly to the wall clock. It was just after two. 'What are *you* doing here?'

'I work here.' Mark's look was snide. 'Remember?'

She gave him a tight, tolerant smile. 'You're back very early.'

Mark shrugged. 'I came off the bike.'

Carol's eyes flared. 'What! Where's your delivery? The packet?' She seemed about to launch herself at him.

Casually, he patted his satchel. 'Here. What's up?'

Carol let out a heavy sigh. 'The client,' she snapped, 'is waiting.'

Mark nodded, and moved to the door. *Don't ask about the bike*, he thought. *Don't ask about me.*

Behind him, he heard Carol's fingers rap impatiently on the desk top. But he was too glad to be leaving to give a damn.

The delivery address was on the third floor of the block. The name on the door read VALUE VIDEO DISTRIBU-TORS. Inside was bright and modern; film bills lined the walls. A typist was hard at work behind the single desk.

'Delivery,' Mark announced.

'Thanks.' The typist paused long enough to take the package, dropping it casually into a crowded IN tray. She was thirtyish, blonde, radiating brisk efficiency. She went straight back to her typing.

Mark hesitated. No one treated sums like this so matter-of-factly, so normally. It didn't make sense.

The woman looked up again, frowning at his continued presence. 'Thank you,' she repeated, firmly.

'Oh, right.' Flustered, Mark turned away. 'Cheerio.'

The staccato of her typing followed him to the lift.

Chapter 10

The flat was at the end of a corridor off a service lift, beyond the last floor of offices. A hole in the front door marked where the lock had been. Even so, Val had to kick the door two or three times to shift rubbish that had accumulated behind it.

'I want you to stay offside for a few days,' he announced, stepping inside.

Following him through the doorway, Christy let out a low whistle of disgust. Jesus, he knew Val was worried about him, but he could have picked a better hideaway than this. Debris littered the bare floor – a rusty gas heater, upturned boxes, scattered rags. The walls had been stripped back to rotting plaster, dark with mould. A damp mustiness pervaded the air.

'Yeah,' Val nodded grimly. 'You could try doing it up a bit, you know. You could try working for a living.'

Christy laughed, and kicked over a box. 'You must be joking.'

Val sighed, and walked to the window. Was Christy being particularly stroppy, or had it not dawned on him that this penthouse dungeon was a punishment?

Things had been going wrong since the jewellery shop raid. Too many people had been whispering. The leaks weren't coming from his end, so it had to be Christy and his contacts. Val could sense bad undercurrents; that made him nervous.

He nodded towards a deep window set in the slope of the ceiling. 'Come on. I'll show you the roof.'

Pushing open the window, they climbed out on to a narrow fire escape. Bare brick and ducting surrounded them. An iron railing guarded a five-storey drop to a small, square yard. Val leaned on the metal.

'I don't like being so close to people, Christy,' he confided. 'Not any more.'

Christy shut the window behind them. 'Because of McGuigan?'

'No.' Val shook his head. He moved along the fire escape. 'McGuigan's on the way out. Things are happening. There's new people coming up.'

He began climbing steps through a concrete archway. On the further side was a door. Christy followed him through on to a broad, open rooftop, punctuated by low skylights and stubby chimney pots. The area was awash with light. The view, to the city limits and beyond, was spectacular.

'Jesus,' Christy murmured.

'Pretty impressive, eh?' Val smiled, pleased with Christy's response. *I take with one hand*, he thought, *I give with the other*.

He allowed his enthusiasm to show. 'I really love it up here. It's so quiet, you know.' They strolled to an elaborate balcony, resting their elbows on the stone edge. A busy junction hummed below them. 'People never imagine you're up here. They never look up. Never!'

Chuckling, Christy leaned forward, miming the action of aiming a weapon. 'You could mount a machine gun up here.' He sprayed the hurrying crowds with phantom bullets, making explosive sounds in the back of his throat.

Val roared with laughter. They were like kids again in Henrietta Street, heaving rotten fruit at the backs of passers-by. 'You're fucking crazy,' Val told him.

His laughter died as he looped an arm over Christy's shoulder. 'I don't like being so close to your friend Danny,' he said. His tone was icy.

50

Christy stared at him, suddenly alert to the danger in Val's eyes; conscious, too, that Val was directly behind him, and the balcony was disconcertingly low.

'He's in town,' Val said. 'He's looking for turn-ons.'

Christy frowned. 'I gave him the gear.'

'Did you?' Val nodded, gazing into the distance. 'Then what did he do with it?' He turned back to Christy, his eyes boring into him.

'I'll find him,' Christy promised.

Val paused, then, as quickly as it had come, the ice vanished. He smiled benevolently, his encircling arm losing its threat. 'I know you will.'

He stepped back from the balcony, drawing Christy with him. 'Don't be so uptight, Christy. Come on down. We'll get you some light bulbs.'

Thoroughly confused, Christy allowed himself to be led away.

Mark's house fascinated Colette. She had wanted to see it simply as a reflection of his personality now, and its neatness immediately impressed her. She knew married men who were not as together as this. But she had forgotten that she had been here before. Probably no more than half a dozen times – generally to pick up Danny. It surprised her how much she remembered. It was like stepping back four years.

'It's exactly the same,' she called out, mounting the stairs.

'What?' Mark called from his bedroom.

'The house.'

'Yeah.' He was standing in his underpants before his wardrobe mirror, combing freshly washed hair. 'I haven't done much with it.'

He became aware of Colette's reflection. She had paused in the doorway, directly behind him, her eyes focussed on the back of his leg. They held a look of frozen vulnerability.

Mark glanced down. A line of bruises extended down his left calf. The resemblance to needle tracks was astonishing.

'I came off the bike the other day,' he said quickly, and saw the relief light up her face. 'Racing.'

Grinning, she came up behind him. 'Speedy Gonzales.' She slipped grateful arms around his waist. They admired each other in the mirror. 'Who were you racing?'

He resumed combing. 'Sharon.'

'Oh yes, the blonde one.' Colette's expression grew arch. 'No wonder you fell off.'

Mark put down his comb and turned to face her, drawing her to him. 'Yeah,' he smiled happily, 'she's beautiful, isn't she?'

He gave a yelp, and avoided her rising knee only by an adroit twist to one side. They began to grapple each other, giggling, until they lost their balance and tumbled back on to the bed. Breathless, Mark propped his head and looked down at Colette, his hand smoothing her stomach.

'You know what I was thinking, don't you?' she said quietly.

'Yeah. And you were wrong.' He glanced where her fingers toyed with his, and his smile faded.

Her presence had ruffled the stillness of the house, invaded it with a new kind of energy, but that energy had also stirred long-hidden memories. He couldn't ignore them any longer.

'How is Danny?' he asked.

He saw Colette's face change. 'The same as ever. Worse even.'

Mark sighed. It confirmed what little he had heard. 'It's all the news these days, isn't it?'

He rolled off the bed and moved to the window, staring down glumly into the darkening street.

'You two used to be like brothers,' Colette said. She got

off the bed to face him directly. 'What happened?'

He looked up at her. 'I stopped using. Danny didn't. It was as if I'd let him down.'

Colette's eyes dropped; she'd had that treatment from her brother; it was nothing she wanted to be reminded of. 'I thought you'd got really cold. When you never asked about him.'

Mark was shaking his head. 'I wanted to get to know you again.' His hand reached out to touch her arm. 'Just us. As we are now.'

'Without Danny?' Colette's voice was a whisper, soft as a betrayal.

'Yeah.' No doubt in his reply.

Her hand rose to stroke his cheek. 'I'm glad,' she admitted.

Chapter 11

The Arctic blue BMW purred to a halt outside VAL'S FOR VALUE. Here, on the shopping centre's walkway, its gleaming presence was both incongruous and illegal, but it was late dusk, and only breeze-blown rubbish stirred beneath the shuttered shop fronts. 'Uncle Val . . . .' Christy spoke softly from the driver's seat. It was like an invocation.

Val detached himself from the shadows beneath his shop entrance. He was dressed all in white, white shoes, white suit, white belted raincoat, white gloves, like a bizarrely fashionable surgeon. Walking quickly, glancing from side to side, he crossed in front of the car and slipped into the front passenger seat.

'How you doing, Val?' Danny spoke from the back seat, his face pale against the cream interior.

'Danny!' Val said, and tapped the steering wheel. 'Bring us over to the new gaff, Christy.'

As the car moved off, he turned to the back. 'We're just going for a little chat, Danny. Going somewhere more comfortable. You'll like it.'

He smiled a broad, warm smile. Danny responded weakly. Beneath the seat back his knuckles were clenched white. Not even Detective Sergeant Dunne had made him as scared as he was now.

Mark came back from the bar with two whiskeys and dry ginger, and placed them on the small table. Colette was twitching so much in her impatience she had lit a cigarette while he'd been gone.

'Come on, tell me!' she hissed. 'What was in the packet?' Her eyes shone with excitement.

Mark grinned. He had been unable to keep silent about his discovery for longer than an hour. Theatrically, he glanced round, though the pub was nearly empty in the early evening. 'Thousands!' he revealed.

Colette chuckled. 'Have you got itchy fingers?'

Mark's eyes widened. 'No way. The money's got to be hot.'

'Why?'

'Does your bank send money around like that?'

Colette grunted her agreement and drew on her cigarette. Mark paused, realising his enthusiasm to share his secret was hardly discreet. That sort of knowledge could well be dangerous. He sipped at his glass. 'In a way,' he said, 'I shouldn't be telling you this.'

'Oh come on.' Colette reached out to touch his hand. 'I like you telling me.'

Mark brightened. 'Tell you what I could do.'

'What?'

'Shop them. Take over the straight business and bring back Speed Couriers.'

Colette smiled, struck by the idea, but even more by Mark's enthusiasm. Danny had always said he was bright. It was good that he didn't see himself riding a bike for ever.

'My own business.' Mark toyed with the thought, then grinned. 'And very legal.'

Rising in the service lift, Val kept up an unceasing flow of smiling affability, rivetting Danny, who took in not one word. At the top Christy led the way down a narrow corridor to the flat's front door, and turned the key in a brand new Yale lock. He stood back to allow Val to enter first, his arm hooked over Danny's shoulder.

'There you go, Danny,' Val beamed, flicking on the light switch. 'As you can see we're in a bit of a mess. Never mind. Take a pew.'

Danny stepped into a broad, desolate room lit by a single unshaded bulb. Walls and ceilings were dark, the floor bare. The only furniture was a wooden chair and a table, holding a radio, newspapers, two light bulbs and several empty lager cans. In a corner was a sleeping bag and a small holdall. Danny went to the chair and sat down.

'Christy's become a deserted father,' Val announced, taking off his raincoat and gloves and handing them to Christy, who laughed. 'You see, Christy's name is on the rent book. We do the flat up, then rent it to a needy family.'

'It's nice,' Danny nodded, his smile weak, his hands pressing hard on his knees.

'Yeah,' Val smiled. He picked up a light bulb from the table, and, playing with it, bent low over Danny. His eyes were soft as he gazed into Danny's face. 'You've been talking to the filth, Danny, haven't you?'

The fear jumped into Danny's eyes. His head was rigid. 'No I haven't, Val. I swear.'

'You know I don't like that, don't you?' Val's voice was a gentle purr, the tone of a disappointed father.

Danny's head shuddered in nervous denial. 'I haven't, Val – honest. Christy?' His eyes flickered across the room, but Christy, his face set, turned away.

'You let me down, Danny,' Val persisted.

'Look, I didn't say nothing to them, Val. I swear – honest.'

'You're sure?'

'You know me, Val. I wouldn't ...' Danny's voice was a strained plea, strangled by despair. 'I swear ....'

Val nodded in understanding, his gaze drinking Danny in, savouring him. His smile was like a benediction, an absolution. 'OK.' He straightened, gently patting Danny's shoulder.

'*Please*, Val . . .' Close to tears, Danny raised his head.

'It's OK.' Val was still nodding, turning away now.

With alarming suddenness, his arm swung back. His free hand still held the light bulb. It smashed against the hard bone above Danny's right eye, the glass splintering and tearing into the eyeball below.

Danny screamed, clutching at Val's hand as it worked the shattered bulb into the socket. Then, breathing deep, Val jerked himself free. Bellowing, Danny clapped both hands to the bloody slit where his eye had been.

Val turned and deposited the remains of the bulb on the table. He pulled a white handkerchief from his trouser pocket and carefully wiped the blood from his hand while he waited for Danny's screams to subside.

'Now Danny,' he said softly, bending to him, 'you see what happens, don't you? Now you *know*.'

He glanced across the room. 'Christy, take care of him, will you?'

Then, with a final regretful glance at Danny, he picked up his white raincoat and gloves, and left the room.

Christy stood mesmerised, both repelled and awed, as Danny's sobs rose to a new crescendo.

'Jesus,' Danny wailed, rocking on his chair. 'Oh – Jesus – Jesus – *fuck*!'

58

Chapter 12

A stiff breeze raised white horses off the beach, but Colette, wrapped as warmly as the baby she bounced on her knee, was oblivious to the chill. 'Ring a ring a rosie,' she cooed. 'Asha, asha, we all fall down.' The baby studied her uncertainly, then broke into a hesitant grin.

'Lovely girl,' Colette hugged her, laughing, and gazed down the strand.

The light was scalding. Two or three hundred yards away, against the water's edge, Mark and Sharon appeared to be lining their bikes up together. As Colette watched, both bikes surged forward, streaking towards her.

For the first hundred yards they came as straight as arrows, first one moving ahead, then the other. Then Mark swerved towards Sharon; Sharon responded. For the last hundred yards they were weaving like snakes, making Colette gasp at their proximity. But it was Sharon who reached her first, skidding to a flashy halt in a spray of sand.

'Nice one,' Colette told her, as she pulled off her helmet and shook her blonde hair free. Mark stopped at her side, grinning wryly as he removed his helmet.

'Thanks,' said Sharon, glancing at him. She turned back to Colette. 'Do you ride?'

Mark raised his eyes skyward as Colette shook her head. 'No.'

Sharon shrugged. 'Must be difficult. Not having the interest like.'

'In bikes?' Colette was surprised.

'Course.'

'I'm more into men, myself.' Colette's grin surfaced slowly, wry and teasing. It was too infectious. Sharon's wind-flushed face broke into a broad smile. 'Fair enough,' she agreed.

Beside her, Mark breathed easier. He had been more concerned than he realised about this encounter. He and Sharon had had their moments of intimacy in the past, but circumstances had conspired to prevent anything more serious developing. Mutual attraction had evolved into friendship. It was not an easy thing to explain.

He coughed to interrupt the flow of rapid conversation. 'Well, girls ...'

The women glanced at each other in mock disbelief. Sharon cocked her head at him. 'Jesus, do you hear this?'

'I don't know, Sharon,' said Colette. 'Some guys ...'

Sharon nodded. 'Can't even win a bleeding race.'

Then both erupted into bright laughter, while Mark gave them a look of pained tolerance.

That morning Christy called Val from a coin box.

'How's the new accommodation?' asked Val.

'Fantastic,' said Christy, 'now I've got light bulbs I can see how big the cockroaches are instead of just feeling them.'

Val laughed. Then his smile changed. He was at the counter in VAL'S FOR VALUE. His fingers plucked at a Stephen King paperback. 'I went too far with Danny, didn't I?'

Christy sounded non-committal. 'A bit ....'

Val drew in breath. 'I shouldn't have been there. I shouldn't have marked him.'

'I dropped him at St Brendan's,' said Christy. 'He knows better than to say anything.'

'Feelings – you shouldn't let your feelings get out of

hand.'

'Nothing wrong with a bit of feeling,' said Christy.

Val laughed again, suddenly. 'You're a good man, Christy. Keep smiling. We'll get you out of there in a couple more days.'

'Thanks,' said Christy dully.

Val put down the phone. He stood quietly a moment, staring at the rows of toys.

With Danny he hadn't blocked an information leak, he'd simply created a man with a grudge, a grudge the kid would remember every time he looked in the mirror. God knows what he'd do when he got enough H inside him.

He'd been a bloody fool. But it shouldn't be too late to put things right. He picked up the phone again and began dialling.

The Norton dated from the early fifties, a gleaming brute of a machine – or at least it had been since Mark had stripped it back to the frame, rebuilding it piece by piece, laying down spray coat after spray coat of bright, glistening paint. It had taken him two years so far, and could take as long again. That didn't matter. It was apart from everything else, a refuge, a labour of love.

Crouching by the light of a shielded light bulb, he adjusted the tension on the clutch cable, squeezing the handlebar control at intervals to judge the result. He was so absorbed he did not realise he was alone until metal scraped on the concrete floor at his back. Startled, he swung the light round. Across the cluttered lean-to, the door to the front garden was open. A figure loomed there, its face waxy and unreal in the yellow light. A large cotton bandage, secured by two tapes, covered the right eye.

'Danny?' Mark whispered.

Danny smiled thinly; he seemed fragile, sheepish. 'How's it going?'

'OK.' Mark got to his feet, clipping the bulb over a handlebar. He felt flummoxed, awkward, not knowing how to react. It had been so long – so much had happened – and what in God's name was that bandage for?

Danny seemed no less certain. He shuffled in, seizing on the bike. 'Bit of a blast from the past, isn't it? Does it go?'

'It will soon. It's vintage.'

Danny nodded. 'That's the old wreck that used to be lying outside? Your Dad's?'

'Yeah.' Mark turned to put down the spanner he had been holding, and tugged at a light pull. A fluorescent tube blinked above their heads; clinical light flooded the small workshop.

'I believe you're knocking around with Colette these days.'

Mark looked back, his hackles stirring. Was that what this was all about? Danny had hardly been the protective brother before. 'News travels fast,' he said stiffly.

'How is she?'

'She's great – she's fine.'

Danny nodded, blinking, as though suddenly at a loss. There was no anger in him, no fraternal jealousy. Mark felt a pang of guilt. The fellow had come to him first, and he was obviously in a very bad way.

'Do you want a cup of tea?' he offered.

Danny's face immediately brightened. 'Yeah.' He sighed gratefully. 'Love one . . . .'

The lean-to abutted the kitchen. Mark crossed to the door and went inside. As he reached for the kettle, Danny followed him to the doorway. 'I'm not disturbing you?' he asked quickly. 'Colette isn't coming round?'

'No, no.' Mark plugged in the kettle, and turned to him with a grin. 'I like the hair.'

'Yeah!' Danny pushed his hand through it carelessly. 'Just a change of image. Didn't work, though.'

'What do you mean?'

'I still got busted. On a stroking charge.'

Mark dropped tea-bags into a couple of mugs. 'Are you getting sent down?'

Danny shook his head. 'The filth offered no charges and a legal dope programme. If I talked about Val Bourke. Do you know him?'

Mark turned from his mugs. The name had arisen in vague gossip. 'I've heard of him.'

'Yeah, well, you know McGuigan in the D.S.?' Mark nodded. 'McGuigan wanted me to keep talking. Val found out.'

A chill rose about Mark's heart. 'Your eye?' he asked softly.

Danny's head bobbed. He swallowed. 'With a light bulb ....' He straightened abruptly. 'Listen, I don't like asking, but is there any way I could crash here tonight?'

Mark gasped. 'You've got some way of asking!'

'Do you think I want to?' Danny snapped. There was an old bitterness in his voice.

The kettle clicked. Mark picked it up and filled the mugs. He glanced up at Danny, suddenly struck by a memory. 'Do you remember the first real stroke you pulled?'

Danny's strained expression relaxed. 'Jesus ...' he grinned. 'Yeah.'

'The jump over in the post office?'

Danny laughed. 'The big time. Fifty old age pension books!'

And me, waiting on the bike outside, thought Mark. *Engine running, scared shitless, waiting to grab the toy gun and the loot.*

He knew why the incident had come back to him. 'That was when I stopped using.' he said.

Danny's smile froze. His face hardened. 'When you didn't have *me* to rob for you.'

Mark shook his head. And it began to move, all the old blockages, all the old pent-up emotion. Four whole years of it. He stepped towards Danny. 'It didn't mean enough to me to snatch from some old postmistress . . . .'

Danny turned away contemptuously. 'You let me down!'

'I didn't let you down, Danny.'

'I couldn't *be* you!'

'I never asked you to be!'

Mark caught Danny's arm, pulling him around. Danny's face was a mask of pain, half obliterated by the massive wad of cotton. His voice cracked. 'Look, I'm blind, man. I'm fucking blinded!' Tears welled in his one good eye. He was clutching at Mark's sleeve.

Appalled, stricken, Mark gripped his arm. 'It's OK,' he whispered.

'It's *not* OK!' Danny shook his head violently. 'These guys are animals. Fucking animals!'

'It's OK.' Mark squeezed his arm. 'You can stay. It's alright.'

Sobbing, Danny fell against his shoulder, his whole body shaking. 'Thanks, Mark, thanks . . . .' They swayed together in the semi-darkness of the kitchen.

Oh Jesus, Danny, thought Mark. *Oh sweet Jesus, what have you done to yourself?*

Chapter 13

They were like two survivors from some vast conflict, long lost comrades in arms, so blasted and battle-weary they no longer remembered, or cared, on which side they had fought. Only the comradeship mattered, nourished by nostalgia and beer and a thread of genuine affection. As they talked into the early hours, it seemed to Mark a time out of time. He had the oddest feeling that he was conversing with the dead – the corpse as much his own as Danny's.

His alarm woke him early. He roused Danny from the spare bedroom, made strong tea and doorsteps of toast, dripping with butter. When he dropped Danny off in Henry Street just before eight thirty, he realised he had said only half of what he had intended. He wanted to prove that it was possible to go on with almost nothing; that almost nothing was more than enough if you let it be. And one day, long after you had stopped thinking about anything but the next tiny step, you would have paid your dues, and something extraordinary could happen. Like Colette.

But, as Danny hopped off the back of the bike, slapping Mark on the back, there was suddenly no more time.

'Thanks a million, man,' Danny grinned, already moving away.

'Hey!' Mark halted him. 'Stay in touch. I might have some work on.'

Danny looked quizzical. 'What sort of work?'

'On the bikes.'

Danny's grin was wry, dismissive. 'Listen, I'll see you.

Places to go.'

His glibness irritated Mark. It was the old Danny again: a good sleep, a good meal, good crack, and the future ceased to exist. It wasn't like that any more. 'Stop giving me these things to do, people to see shit!' Mark snapped.

Danny's grin died. 'OK.' He raised a defensive hand. 'I *said* I'll be in touch.'

Mark nodded. Danny's smile reappeared. He winked, and slapped Mark's shoulder. Then he was gone, shoulders hunched, hands in pockets, stalking through the busy crowd, lost to sight in seconds.

Mark let out a gentle sigh. He hadn't run out of time this morning. He had let it happen four years ago when Danny might still have listened to him.

He stamped on the kick-start, and pulled away.

A breather, Danny told himself. That was all he had needed. A little respite to sort himself out.

Colette had been right – Mark was OK. Changed and straight, with all the wildness gone from him, but there was something solid and decent at bottom. It had been there from the beginning, awed into quiescence by Danny the big man, Danny the guy who pulled the shots.

Danny had always envied it. It represented strength, a strength he couldn't match. Colette could lean on that. Walking fast, he grunted to himself, derisively. She'd need it after the merry dance he'd led her these past years.

But all that was over now. Now he had to get away – to England, to the North, anywhere. Because, sure as hell, Val and McGuigan both would grind him between them until only a husk remained. But first, just to steady himself, he'd need a good score.

He ducked into the first empty phone kiosk he found, and began dialling.

It was just before twelve thirty, and Mark was looking forward to a lunchtime roll and a cup of tea when Carol gave him the message. Another pick-up from Value Video for the editing warehouse, with a return package waiting.

Danny's visit had pushed the hot money incident from his mind. It would be a chance to see if the previous run had been an isolated incident, a chance to find out what was really going on. Galvanised, he was at the office block in minutes.

The package lay in the OUT tray. The blonde typist was at work behind her desk. She glanced up briefly. 'The address is on the front.'

'Yeah – I know.' Mark smiled behind his visor, squeezing a faint response from the woman. She went on with her typing.

Outside, he slipped the package into his satchel, and checked his watch. Twelve forty-five. He could use the excuse of lunchtime traffic – if he had to. He started the bike, and headed for home. He managed it by one, bumping the bike on to the concrete in front of the lean-to, and quickly thumbed his radiophone.

'Carol? I'm taking a lunchbreak.'

There was a crackle of static. 'OK. Two o'clock.'

'Right.'

He propped the bike and hurried to the front door. In the kitchen he dropped his helmet on the table, and sat down, placing the packet in front of him. It looked exactly the same as the broken one, light brown, anonymous, the flap self-sealing.

He breathed in, and turned to pick a motorcycle points measure off the dresser. He was going to look damn silly if the other packet had been a one-off – someone settling a debt in panic. Selecting a measure, he slipped its point under the flap and gently began to sever the strands of glue. In a minute the flap lifted. He up-ended the packet.

Two, three, four, then five transparent plastic envelopes dropped on to the table top. Each contained pure white powder. Mark gazed at them, hypnotised. If this were not smack it was the wildest coincidence he had ever encountered.

'Three-two-four, Mark!' The radiophone spat the words, making Mark start. Annoyed, he snapped off the machine, turned and snatched a pair of kitchen scales off the dresser. Setting it before him, he began to drop the plastic envelopes one by one onto the weighing tray.

The hand jerked around the dial. Two ounces, four, six. 'Jesus,' he murmured. There was nearly half a pound of the stuff. If it *was* heroin, he had never seen so much before in his life.

His eyes rose to the kitchen clock. One ten.

He began stuffing the envelopes back into the packet. But with the last he paused. He turned to the dresser again, pulled open a drawer, and began rummaging inside. In a moment he found what he wanted – a small plastic container of film. Levering off the top, he dropped the unused film back in the drawer. Then he put the empty container on the table top, lifted up the points measure and carefully opened the re-sealable lip of the envelope.

He took as much powder as he dared, barely enough to cover the nail of his smallest finger, shook it into the film container, and replaced the cap. Then he smoothed his finger along the lip of the envelope, re-sealing it. He pushed it back into the packet. A scattering of white grains still clung to the measure. He stared at it for a long moment.

Four years since his last hit. Three years, seven months and about two weeks, to be exact. And he had been very exact.

There was no other way to be sure. He put out his tongue and ran the end of the measure along the tip. The taste was unmistakable.

The telephone erupted into violent sound.

Mark was suddenly spitting, choking, heaving himself up out of his chair, rubbing his leather sleeve backwards and forwards across his mouth to rid himself of every lingering grain. *These guys are animals, Mark. They're fucking animals!*

His heart crashing, he went through into the hallway. The telephone rested on a coat-stand, just back from the frosted glass of the front door. He took a breath and picked up the receiver. 'Hello?'

'How you doing, sunshine?' Colette's voice flooded the world with light and relief. As he replied, he heard his voice shake. 'Colette. I was going to call over this evening.'

He heard her chuckle of pleasure. 'Did you send me this rose?'

He grinned. He'd forgotten. He'd seen the service in a shop window next to a call the day before, obeyed a sudden impulse. 'Do you like it?'

'It's beautiful,' she purred. 'I just didn't think it was your style.'

Mark laughed. 'Man of mystery, that's me. Never know what I'll do next. Listen . . .' he glanced toward the kitchen door. 'What's your bank like with loans?'

'Loans?' She sounded surprised. 'What for?'

'A business.'

'You'll need capital.'

Mark nodded. 'A house is capital. And I've got a couple of hundred saved.'

Colette's tone changed, became businesslike. 'Are you serious? About a courier company?'

'Yeah.' Hearing himself say it surprised him; did he really mean it? Or was he just sounding brave because he felt so much the opposite? 'Only when I'm ready,' he went on. 'I have to get back to work.'

'See you, love.'

'I'll give you a call later.' He put down the receiver.

So many things happening at once. So much to risk. So much to gain. He hurried back into the kitchen.

Chapter 14

Danny slammed down the receiver and swore, grinding his knuckles against the call-box wall. What had happened? Had that maniac Val put the word out on him? Was that why he couldn't score – was the evil bastard punishing him some more?

He stared up the street towards Mountjoy Square. The unmarked Garda car was still parked on the corner, perfectly positioned to spot the front door to his bedsit. It was that Dunne guy in the driver's seat, had been since early afternoon. Christ, you'd think they'd be more subtle than that. That wasn't a face he'd forget easily.

Danny bumped his head against the cracked glass, wracking his brains for more numbers. *Somebody* had to be dealing in this city. Not everyone could be in Val Bourke's pocket.

But there was only one number left uncalled. Was this what Val wanted? Did he want him to beg? He began dialling. It was a Kincora number. It was a long time before a woman answered.

'Mary? It's Danny Adams. You know, Christy's friend. I'm in a bit of a fix.'

The woman's voice sounded distant, slurred. He realised she must have just shot up, heavily too. It was an effort to make her understand.

'I don't know if Val'd be too pleased – he's getting funny about the good stuff ....' The words crawled uphill from a million miles away. He was terrified she'd simply black out.

'Anything, Mary! Never mind the H – anything you've

got. I'm not fussed. I just need a buzz. Val doesn't have to know . . . .' He winced, biting back the last words, willing her not to take them in. The silence was agonising.

'Mary?'

Then, thankfully, came her long sigh. 'I might have some coke.'

'Great! Fantastic!' He thumped the window glass in joy. 'It'll cost . . .'

'No problem – any price – it's yours.'

'Give me an hour.'

The phone went dead. Danny put the receiver back, and stood gripping the hard plastic, his joy evaporating, riddled by a thousand buzzing doubts. She *had* to remember; she *mustn't* pass out; she must be telling the truth!

With a sick sigh, he backed from the box. He had to keep walking to stop trembling. He cast a last, pained glance at the waiting Garda car, and headed back toward the city centre.

Fifty yards away Detective Sergeant Dunne picked up his radio microphone. 'He's stopped pissing about at the phone box. He's heading your way.'

'Fine.' McGuigan's voice rasped from the speaker. 'Go on and get yourself some lunch. Leave your radio on.'

'You can't miss him,' Dunne added. 'He's hurt his eye.' He grunted. 'Probably walked into something when he was spaced out.'

It struck Mark as ironic that he had never been to this place before. He had used for nine months, and gone through a withdrawal hell he could still barely remember, but he had done it alone, locking himself away in a house of the dead. He hadn't even enlisted the help of the family's doctor, let alone a proper drug dependency unit like this. Did that make him stupid, or brave? Had he made it seem *easy*? No wonder Danny had resented him so much.

And yet the unit looked entirely ordinary, no different from a thousand other hospital waiting rooms, white-painted and smelling of disinfectant and fresh polish. Even the AIDS posters, screaming their warnings against shared needles, could have adorned a dozen other walls. He became aware of activity behind the window of the office at the far end. The middle-aged staff nurse was talking to a doctor, a slim, thin-faced man in his fifties, so tall his stoop seemed permanent. He nodded as the nurse handed him a sheaf of papers, then glanced out at Mark.

A moment later he emerged, raising his eyes to Mark and indicating a plain door to one side. 'Come inside, will you?'

'Thanks.' Mark followed him into a tiny room, almost filled by a table, two chairs and a couch pushed against a wall. The doctor squeezed himself behind the table, dropping papers on top, then leaned forward across them, and steepled his hands. Mark sat down opposite him.

There was a moment's pause while the man seemed to collect his thoughts. 'At this hospital,' he said at last, 'we treat addiction. We do not wish to see our substance analysis service used for – quality control . . . .' The edge in his voice was unmistakable; he clearly thought Mark was an addict, or a dealer.

'I've already explained,' Mark said quickly. 'I found this – substance – in my brother's bedroom.'

'This substance,' the doctor said smoothly, glancing down at his papers, 'isn't just heroin. It's the purest heroin we have ever seen outside a laboratory.' He raised his eyes to Mark. 'Your "brother" – ' a slight pause suggested his disbelief – 'is dealing with very serious people.'

I shouldn't have come, Mark thought. *I've been a bloody fool. He's going to blow the whole thing wide-open.* He could only pursue the charade to the end.

'What do you suggest?' he asked.

The doctor was now staring hard at him. 'I cannot

recommend treatment strongly enough, before your brother does any more damage.'

Mark nodded, his heart bumping. 'I'll talk to him.' He got up, moving quickly, expecting to be called back immediately. But the doctor did not stir.

'I have,' he said, 'fourteen-year-old patients snatching handbags to buy what you just brought in here.' He was gazing into the middle distance, face creased with concern, Mark apparently forgotten.

Mark stared at him. The official manner had thrown him. The guy wasn't interested in punishment, or blame, only cure. 'You do methadone programmes here, don't you?' Mark spoke hesitantly.

'Yes.' The doctor nodded, and straightened, as though pulling himself together. Official again. 'We are the only licensed hospital.'

'Yeah. OK.' Mark smiled thinly. 'Well – thanks.'

He was through the door before the doctor had a chance to respond.

Danny hung back in the entrance to the burger bar, hopping from foot to foot, clenching his fists in his jacket pockets. It was too bloody good to be true. No one would come all the way from Kincora just to help him out, even for the money he was offering. Shit, if she didn't, he'd run straight out into Aungier Street, flatten himself under the first corporation bus. Grinding his teeth together, he did not notice the taxi sliding along the kerb to his right.

'Danny?'

He looked up in surprise. Mary's wan face showed through an open window in the back.

'Jesus!' Unable to prevent himself grinning inanely, he hurried to the kerbside.

She reached out a small folded square of silver foil, and pressed it into his palm. 'It's all I could manage.'

'You're an angel! You're a wonder!' Gasping, he pushed a tube of notes through the window.

The window slid upwards, masking Mary's face. The taxi eased away. Breathing deep breaths of relief, Danny glanced up and down the street. No one there who shouldn't be. Now he'd need somewhere quiet, private, and the damn pubs were still shut from lunchtime. He began walking, fast.

An accordian player was grinding out a song on a corner of Camden Street, a sandy-haired leprechaun of a figure, dark-suited and broken-voiced. Passing on the opposite pavement, Danny gave him scant notice, until a new Ford appeared from the side street at the man's back and eased gently to a halt, not bothering to turn into the main road.

There was something odd about the figure in the front passenger seat. The man sitting there was holding his hand to his mouth. Then the light patterns shifted on the windscreen, and Danny recognised the radio microphone of an unmarked Garda car. The man in the front seat was McGuigan.

'*Shit*!' Panic reared in him like a mad beast. His only thought was flight. Blindly he spun round, and found himself facing the doors of a pub. Seeing nothing, he pushed inside.

It was an old Victorian bar, etched glass at the windows, dark moulded wood and a long, marble counter. A young barman in shirt sleeves stood behind it, polishing glasses. There was no one else in the place.

Panting, Danny stared about him. There seemed only the one door. Then he became aware of the barman's curious gaze. He gabbled the first words that sprang into his head. 'Scotch and red.'

The barman nodded at his bandage, frowning sympathetically. 'Car crash?'

'What?'

The barman raised a finger to his own eye.

'Oh yeah – I mean, no!'

Danny spun, eyes jumping, as a customer appeared behind him, rising from a stairway to the toilets. Apprehensive, the man stepped back. Without a word, Danny plunged down the stairs. The customer raised baffled eyes, and reclaimed his glass at the counter.

'Joy rider,' the barman grunted. The customer shook his head, and drank.

The stairs led only to the toilets – a narrow, cramped room, white-tiled and spartan, electric-lit with no visible windows. Sighing, Danny pushed the door of the single cubicle. Inside was grey and dingy, an L-shaped space half the size of the main room. No window. No escape. He didn't care. He needed to recoup; he needed to hide. Most of all he needed his turn-on.

He squeezed inside, slipping the bolt and rifling in his pocket for Mary's silver foil. The powder it contained was white and compressed, almost an inch square – much more than he'd expected. Gratefully he brought the foil up to his nose, blocked a nostril with his thumb and inhaled sharply.

He sighed as the tingling struck his nasal passages. It was good stuff – bloody good – better than he'd had in a long time. There was already a pleasant numbness between his eyes. Breathing deep, feeling the jagged edges of his nerves soften and relax, he picked his way along the tiled wall, turned and sank on to the toilet seat. The buzz was spreading now, assuaging his panic; a kind of dulled normality was returning. His brain began to work again.

What did it matter if McGuigan picked him up again? He could spin him a line, claim Val was planning something, insist he'd know more in a day or two. McGuigan would swallow it – the old bastard was so mad for Val he'd swallow anything. Time – that's what he'd buy. Time to get away, time to put things straight. He'd try London – he had friends there. Perhaps, later on, Colette might join him. Colette and Mark – why not?

He breathed deep again, resting his head against the tiles as the chemical glow warmed him. He realised the cubicle was not unlit, as he had thought. Daylight filtered through a square of cobbled glass above the door. A mottled shaft lit his face.

As he raised his head to it, something heavy and sharp ripped through his stomach. The sensation was so massive and swift he was too shocked to react, even to feel pain. Then it came again, even fiercer, clawing the air from his lungs, and the agony almost knocked him unconscious. His whole body jerked in violent spasm. Suddenly there were cramps in every limb, molten lead in his belly, a screaming in his head.

Terrified, he clutched at the cistern pipe as another spasm convulsed him. His body was running riot; his lungs would not take air. The cistern pipe tore from its mounting; water sprayed across his face. His last coherent thought was, *Colette*. ...

McGuigan walked into the bar and frowned at the two men occupying it. He had thought there was no handy rear exit, but Danny had looked in a mood to leap through windows. Then he caught sight of the staircase. As the barman glanced at him interrogatively, he clattered down the stairs.

The urinal was empty. The cistern in the cubicle was flushing. Water was seeping under the door.

'Danny!' McGuigan shouted, abruptly fearful.

Bending, he struggled to see under the door, but it was too low. He began kicking at the door. Behind him there were footsteps on the stairs, the barman's angry shout. As the lock gave, McGuigan used his full weight on the panel. The door burst inwards.

Danny lay between the toilet seat and the tiled wall,

water splashing from the cistern on to the right side of his head. His face was blue, his good eye staring sightlessly ahead; bloodied and sodden, the bandage hung down on his cheek, exposing the mess of his damaged eye.

'Jesus,' whispered a voice at McGuigan's side. The barman glanced at the gaunt and silent figure of the policeman. 'Who are you?' he cried.

'I'm the police,' said McGuigan thickly, and turned away.

There was a call box some forty yards along the street from the pub. From inside Mary had a clear view of the entrance, the car parked opposite and McGuigan striding across the intervening junction. She was already dialling as the policeman reached into the car, grabbed his radio microphone and began requesting assistance.

'Val,' she said, when the receiver was picked up. 'Danny took his turn on.'

She rang off without waiting for a reply. Across the street McGuigan bawled suddenly at the accordian player on the corner, shocking the small man into silence with a ferocity that seemed quite unnecessary.

Chapter 15

It was nearing dusk when Mark got back from the hospital. He had intended to go home and change before telephoning Colette, but he had too much to tell her, and the evening was half gone already. Only pausing to dump his courier gear at Marino, he followed the back streets the two miles to Colette's address.

She lived in a neat suburban avenue, broader, leafier and generally more prosperous than Mark's. The address, he noted drily, had made Danny's fall from grace all the more unacceptable to his parents.

He was puzzled to notice the living-room curtains drawn: it was hardly dark enough for it yet. Then, when he had pressed the front door bell three times without result, he stepped back to see that the curtains of every other window were drawn too. Colette had not mentioned the family would be going out; he had promised her he would be calling.

Confused, and starting to feel annoyed, he turned for the gate, and caught sight of an elderly woman standing, watching him, in the neighbouring front garden. The blatancy of her curiosity irritated him, and he started for his bike, until the woman called suddenly, 'Is it the Adams's you're looking for?'

Mark stopped and looked at her. She had glasses, her arms folded tightly over a shapeless grey cardigan. 'I might be.'

'They'll be at the hospital now.'

'Hospital?' Mark frowned.

'To identify the boy – the Garda sent a car.' The woman shook her head. 'I feel so sorry for Mrs Adams. To lose someone so young . . . .'

'Lose?' Mark snapped. 'What are you talking about?'

'The son – little Daniel.' The woman's bosom lifted in a sigh. 'He was on the drugs, you know. It's not something you talk about, but it always kills them in the end – it's well known.'

Mark was running for his bike.

'Do you know the family?' the woman called after him. 'I don't mean to pry!'

But the roar of the Suzuki's engine drowned her out.

They were not at St Brendan's or St Lawrence's, Mater Misericordiae or St Patrick's. 'It sounds like a police matter,' a sympathetic receptionist told him. 'Have you talked to the Garda?'

From a coin box outside St Patrick's he rang Colette's home. It was his fifth try in two hours. A voice he didn't know answered.

'Who's that?'

'This is Pat Adams, Kevin's brother.'

'Can I speak to Colette?'

'She's too upset to come to the phone. The doctor's given her something.'

'What's happened to Danný?'

'I'm sorry, are you a friend of the family?'

'Just tell me!'

There was a pause. 'Daniel passed away this afternoon. Can I take your name?'

He slammed down the receiver, lifted it and slammed it again, grinding it into its cradle. When he lifted his head again, his eyes were red-rimmed. They came to focus on a pub front a few doors away.

He drank steadily, not for solace or comfort but

oblivion. But the alcohol only seemed to sharpen his senses. *I abandoned him this morning. I gave up, just like I gave up on him four years ago.* And after a night when they'd been as close as they ever were.

He *knew* Danny would be scoring; it was written all over his face – he'd been strung out, he'd said so – as if Mark could ever have mistaken the signs. Danny would have grabbed anything, anything for a buzz, even if it killed him . . . . And this afternoon he'd been within an inch of giving Danny's name to the drug unit. And bottled out.

Danny the big man; Danny the tough guy. He'd believed it because it suited him, because it denied his own strength, the strength to look after number one. A strength Danny never had. He'd let Danny down.

He'd let Danny down.

It was the fourth or the fifth or the sixth bar, a sprawling, low-ceilinged place, red-lit, throbbing with a solid beat, packed to capacity. To catcalls and cheers a girl danced on a low stage. A crop-haired brunette, she was built for comfort rather than speed, her heavy bosom tenuously sheathed in a see-through top, fleshy thighs pumping inside stockings, suspenders and basque. Deliberately Mark ignored her. Pushing his way through the noise and the smoke, jogging the elbows of customers too drunk or too slow to take offence, he aimed for the bar.

It was all but empty, deserted after last orders. A barman with a hard, blotchy face wiped the bar top. Mark slapped his hand on the damp laminate. 'Give us a drink!'

The barman ignored him.

'I said give us a drink!'

The man turned his back.

Mark snatched up an empty glass and hurled it into the bottles of spirits arrayed at the back of the bar. Before the shattered glass had reached the floor, the barman was vaulting over the bar top. He grabbed Mark's arm and slammed him against the counter. As if by magic a second barman appeared, clutching his other arm.

Struggling wildly, Mark was frog-marched swiftly across the front of the stage, kneed in the stomach, then flung head first against a pair of fire doors. At first he simply bounced of, but at the second attempt his cheek struck the safety bar, and the doors burst open.

He found himself rolling in a dank alleyway between empty beer crates and overflowing dustbins. Slowly, feeling his face, relishing the pain, he climbed to his feet. After a moment he stumbled away towards the nearest street lamps.

I let you down, Danny, I let you down ....

Chapter 16

The cemetery clung to the hillside overlooking Sutton Creek, separated from the broad channel by a scattering of suburban homes. In the clear sunlight of mid-morning the distant water was a pale, inviting blue.

'Hail Mary, full of grace, the Lord is with thee, blessed are thee amongst women and blessed is the fruit of thy womb . . . .' The priest's gabbled intonation rose into the air, muffled by the rumble of a passing jet.

John Patrick McGuigan turned from the view to the small gathering at the graveside. He stood opposite them, ten or twelve feet away, to indicate both his separation from the family group, and his semi-official involvement. Already one of the men had moved across to touch his arm briefly in appreciation of his attendance. The irony of the gesture had not been lost on the policeman.

He was in trouble – not just with his superiors for releasing a suspect with more than reasonable evidence stacked against him; McGuigan was too old a hand to let that worry him. Much more importantly he was at odds with his own view of himself.

His judgement had been wrong, warped by his obsession with Bourke. The boy had been too far gone; he'd seen that, and deliberately ignored it. Danny should have been clapped inside with any charge that stuck, anything to get him off the streets, off the smack and into a special unit. Instead McGuigan had pushed, and pushed – with the inevitable result.

Perhaps the city hadn't changed over these years.

Perhaps he had. And he'd despised Dunne for his Action Man approach. God! By comparison the man was a saint.

He became aware of a young Garda at his side. 'We've got the lab report, sir.'

'Yes?' McGuigan spoke without moving.

'Strychnine.' The Garda grunted in amusement. 'That's one they haven't taught us about – not yet at any rate.'

McGuigan turned to him slowly. 'Rat poison.' The savagery of his tone dashed the amusement from the young man's face. 'For *rats*.'

Thrown, the Garda blinked rapidly as McGuigan looked back at the funeral party. Danny's mother and father were casting handfuls of earth into the open grave, but one pair of eyes was not gazing downward. They belonged to a young man in jeans and a black leather jacket who stood close by the daughter of the family. He was staring straight at McGuigan, his look cold and questioning.

The face looked familiar. McGuigan racked his memory. Yes, three, four years ago. The first time he'd come across Danny. Suspicion of a post office hold-up. One of Adams' associates. Someone who'd ridden a bike for the getaway, and this fellow – name forgotten – had been a courier. But nothing had stuck, and the youngster had faded from view. Learned his lesson perhaps?

What did his look *mean*?

Mark stepped back from the small family group, leaving Colette to support her mother as the ceremony moved to its conclusion. The sight of McGuigan had stirred a resentment the funeral had almost numbed; he had been overcome by a sudden sense of futility.

He had said his goodbyes to Danny that morning a few days ago, and, more properly, in the drunken rage that had followed. Let the family get what they could from the formalities; they'd had little else from Danny recently. He wandered away through the gravestones, choosing paths, it seemed, at random.

Why was McGuigan here? Had he come to gloat? He remembered his one interview with the man so many years before. A cold dank room that could have been a cell. They had kept him waiting for hours, quaking in the fear that they knew everything, the jumpover, the getaway, the loot he'd refused to touch, the smack it had bought, which he had still shared . . . . And then, suddenly, there was the great man. The senior detective, with the soft, silky voice, the smoothly sympathetic manner, offering tea and toffees – as if he were a big kid – offering freedom, offering absolution, if he would just unburden himself, let drop the tiniest, the least significant snippet of information – now what harm could it do, son?

But the freedom McGuigan offered wasn't any freedom Mark wanted. It was the freedom of the cleansed conscience, the unburdened soul, and against that the judicial punishment that would inevitably follow was a small price to pay. Mark had never been more terrified in his life. Only that terror had kept his mouth shut, and saved him.

But Danny hadn't felt that, or thought of terrors much worse. He had listened to that soft, silky voice, had trusted it. And the man had sent him straight out as live bait for Val Bourke. Christ, Bourke had only ripped his eye out – not his bloody soul!

He found he had stopped in front of a simple basalt gravestone, and realised who he had been talking to. IN LOVING MEMORY, he read, SARAH WILSON R.I.P. DIED 19 MARCH 1975. JOHN WILSON BELOVED HUSBAND OF SARAH DIED 6 MAY 1984.

Would any of this have happened if they had still been alive? Danny's parents had not stopped him; it had only been Colette he listened to, and then not enough.

He heard a soft footfall to one side.

'This must bring it all back.' Colette's tone was gentle, her hand a light pressure on his back.

'Yeah.' Mark grunted. 'I keep losing people.'

Colette's hand rose to his shoulder, squeezing it. 'Thanks for coming.'

'Not at all. Anytime.' He turned, catching her shy grin and mirroring it as he realised what he had said. 'You know what I mean.'

She was dressed in black, black jacket, black blouse, black skirt; grief had given her face a waxy smoothness, sharpened the grey of her eyes; he had never seen her look more beautiful. He wanted to crush her to him, but the magnitude of her loss made him awkward. Instead he lifted his gaze towards the distant funeral party, now retreating to the waiting cars.

'What's McGuigan doing here?' he asked.

Her fingers worked at his shoulder. 'He brought the news. He knew Danny for years.'

While Mark absorbed this, she paused, and then gave a heavy sigh. 'Come on – let's get out of here.'

Mark looked at her in surprise. 'Can you?'

She nodded, thinking of hushed conversations with relatives she hardly knew, the clink of tea cups, the discreet splash of whiskey, of parents as baffled and embarrassed by Danny's death as by his life.

'Yeah,' she said quickly, tugging at Mark's waist. 'Come on.'

She sat silently on Mark's bed, gazing at a postcard she had unearthed from her shoulder bag. From the armchair opposite Mark watched her, wanting to share her pain, not wanting to intrude. 'I found this this morning,' she said at last. 'It was when he went to London.'

She handed the postcard to Mark. It was a view of

Trafalgar Square. On the back he read in Danny's scrawling hand: 'Got a girlfriend, a job and a flat. Very happy. *Very* clean.'

Mark handed it back. 'There was a lot of love there,' he said quietly.

Colette nodded. 'At times,' she said, 'I thought he was comparing other girls to me.' She looked up at Mark, her grin fragile and uncertain. 'Like I was some sort of ideal woman.'

The anguish in her face broke Mark's reserve. He moved to her side, slipping his arm around her. 'Yeah,' he murmured. 'Funerals are funny.'

Her face lifted to him. 'You didn't cry . . . .'

Mark's head shook briefly. He looked away.

'What about your father's?'

'No. Not till afterwards.' Now he looked at her. 'Danny came up to the house and got me pissed. He kept me up all night, talking and talking until he got me to cry.'

Colette was smiling, surprised at the memory, pleased to share it. 'Danny did?'

'Yeah.' Slowly Mark's own smile faded, driven out by fresher, less savoury memories.

'What did McGuigan say about Danny's eye?' he asked.

Colette shrugged lightly. 'He didn't know about it.'

She shuddered at the thought. The hospital had mentioned something about a recent accident – so recent Danny had not even bothered to tell her. She could still feel hurt about that.

Then she noticed Mark's expression had darkened. There was a tension in him that suddenly frightened her. 'What?' she prompted. 'Mark, what is it?'

He drew in breath. 'McGuigan used him. For information.'

'What?'

'Danny called here a few nights ago.'

'Danny was *here*?'

'Yeah.' Mark nodded. 'It was good – we talked a lot.'

Colette was trembling, her face working in disbelief, and then horror as the implications multiplied in her mind.

'But – you're telling me he was *murdered*? No – ' she shook her head. 'McGuigan couldn't have known.'

'He knew what he was doing.' Mark spoke flatly.

'No – oh, no . . .' Colette's breath was coming in sharp gulps, her head falling against his shoulder. Then she sprang upright. 'That bastard even gave me his phone number to ring him. Even when he knew what he'd done!'

Her head sank back against Mark's chest, and now the tears came, deep, racking sobs that clawed at his heart.

'Oh Danny, Danny!' Colette cried.

Mark held her tightly, staring sightlessly at the blank wall. He had let Danny down, but he had not lied, he had not cheated, he had not sent him callously to his death. There would be a price to pay for that, a price as heavy as Colette's grief. He promised himself that.

Chapter 17

He was forming a plan, without details, without direction, with only a desperate need to *act*. His last night with Danny had furnished him with names and places, half obliterated by too much beer. In the meantime he had the video company-editing warehouse run. It was his one sure connection with the smack scene – every contact he had had from the old days was long gone.

Something had to break there, something would show the way to go. He began haunting the city centre, taking more than his share of the short, small, low-paying deliveries, making sure he was close to base around half twelve when Value Video had called before. Within two days he struck lucky.

The call came at one, interrupting his sandwiches. He surprised Carol by going immediately.

He found the young video editor seated at his console, fingers flashing over the keys, eyes dancing from monitor to monitor. He might not have moved since Mark's last visit. Only his shirt had changed.

'Nice,' Mark remarked, dropping his package on the desk and glancing at the screens.

A heavy metal band were pounding out a song in a punk version of Dante's *Inferno*. Flames writhed on the walls; extras writhed on the floor.

'Great bodies. Great rhythm,' the editor hissed. Without lowering his gaze, he lifted the return packed from the desk top and slapped it against his shoulder. Mark took it from him.

'You got everything in here, man,' the editor enthused. 'Cross dressed, flat chest, gender bender, bondage – know what I mean?'

Mark grunted non-committally. The man's mania no longer seemed so engaging.

'All day, every day – the video never sleeps, man.' The editor's eyes glinted with reflected images. 'The video never sleeps.'

Unnoticed, Mark made his exit.

The blonde typist at Value Video clearly took a late lunch break. She was typing rapidly when he entered. Today she seemed less severe than usual, even lavishing a brief smile on Mark as she paused to sign his receipt pad.

Retrieving it, he noticed a door half open to the left of her desk. He caught sight of a lurid video display, the end of a broad picture window, overlooking the city. As he moved back to the outer door, the typist called, 'Val?'

His hand on the door handle, Mark froze momentarily. He heard a man's heavy tread, a casual, 'Yeah? Oh, thanks, love.'

Snapping down his visor, Mark turned his head. A man in his late thirties, heavy, hook-nosed, darkly handsome, was leaning over the typist's machine, playfully tapping two of the keys. The blonde gave him a look of pained tolerance. Then, grinning, he glanced up, but the door was already closing on Mark.

Wiping the last traces of shaving soap from his face, Christy emerged from the small washroom and toilet which adjoined Val's office. Val appeared from the outer office, beaming brightly, and immediately tossed a small packet towards him. Christy snatched it out of the air without thought, letting his towel drop.

'There you go!' Val grinned. 'Back on stream.'

'Nice one, Val.' Christy returned the grin and bent for his towel.

It was a change to see Val in a good mood again. It had been a dirty business with Danny; in Christy's view, something as serious as a topping should be done face to face, if at all possible; even a junkie deserved that. But he couldn't deny that Val's solution had been highly effective. Perhaps now he might be allowed to abandon his rooftop refuge. He was getting mighty sick of a cold water flat with a bathroom that was only fit for cockroaches.

Val snatched Christy's jacket from the back of a chair, and held it out to him. 'Come on,' he winked. 'Let's give you a proper wash down. I can smell that flat on you.'

Returning him an old-fashioned look, Christy shrugged on the jacket.

They nodded to the typist and took the lift to the basement carpark, Val tossing over the car keys as they crossed the dimly lit concrete to the BMW.

'No more work for junkies, Christy,' he announced. 'Not any more. If you can't do the time you don't play the game. Danny killed himself, you know.' He stared across the car roof as Christy unlocked the driver's door. 'He should have known better.'

Then you should have topped him in the flat, straight off, Christy thought. *Not blinded the poor bastard*. But he said nothing, simply slid behind the wheel and leaned over to open the passenger door. He was beginning to resent Val's needling. The incident was closed; let it die with the kid. But he knew Val too well to make an issue of it.

'Three-two-four, Mark. Three-two-four, Mark!' Even the distorted tones of the radiophone were sufficient to convey Carol's irritation. She had been calling solidly for nearly two minutes now. Irritated himself, Mark switched off the set.

Damn the woman. There was no way she didn't know what was going on, no way she didn't take her share of the blame.

He settled himself more comfortably on his saddle. A section of roadworks opposite Value Video's block kept him out of sight of the entrance, gave him a clear view through the main glass doors. Value Video, run by Val Bourke: it made such perfect sense, he was surprised it had never occurred to him before. There had to be a direct connection with D-Day Couriers too; establishing that would be his next task.

But right now it was Bourke himself who mattered. He'd wait here all night if necessary. He wanted to see that face again, look into the eyes of a man who got his kicks out of grinding broken light bulbs into other people's faces. He wanted to know the man thoroughly, his friends, his haunts, his habits, the way a hunter learned to know his prey.

A light blue BMW slipped out of a side road to the right of the building, and halted for a gap in the traffic. Finding one, it swung past Mark and accelerated away down the broad street. Startled, Mark kicked down on his starter. Jesus, he had almost missed him. The predatory profile in the front passenger seat. There had to be a carpark at the rear of the block.

Wrenching the throttle, he pulled out into the traffic flow, praying the BMW would not get a clear run. He need not have worried. Though he failed to beat it to the next lights, it slowed just across the junction, and eased into the kerb. Val Bourke got out, carried a small pouch hurriedly to the night safe of a bank, deposited it and climbed back into the car. Mark grunted. Takings so hot he couldn't even wait for the banks to open for the afternoon.

Then, just in time, the lights changed. The car was moving south, toward the city centre, snaring itself so quickly in the dense traffic that Mark soon found himself directly behind, perched on its offside. Its sudden turn to the left surprised him.

He had no choice but to ride on, and slide into the kerb. The traffic was too heavy to swing easily in a circle. He dismounted, and walked the bike back along the pavement.

The BMW had vanished down a narrow alleyway; at the bottom parked cars were visible, what appeared to be a yard, broadening out. Mark remounted and rode on slowly.

The yard was cobbled, lined with cars and vans and light lorries; nondescript buildings rose on either side, fire doors and rear exits. Only one doorway was open, an anonymous stairway rising beneath a raised steel shutter. The BMW was parked next to it. As Mark rode past he saw a small aluminium plaque set in the brickwork. It read, THE BODY CLUB.

Christy was in and out of the sauna within ten minutes. He had no objection to saunas in principle – any aspect of the good life was fine by him, and, by God, he needed to sweat the filth of that flat out of himself – but the club made him nervous. Too many guys preening themselves, admiring each other's bodies beautiful. Too many sly, sidelong glances in the showers. Christ, he'd never been able to stomach gays in the choky; he didn't have to pay a fortune to enjoy their company now. It was a side of Val's life Christy had kept strictly at arm's length. He could understand the man's need for violence, but not this.

He was sitting on a bench in the changing room, fully dressed, when Val sauntered through, whistling cheerfully. Christy waited while he towelled himself, slipped on pants and trousers and began combing his hair in the wall mirror.

'Here, Christy,' Val said at last, 'give my back a rub, will you?' Laying down his comb, he offering his broad, bare shoulders to the seated man. Christy rose reluctantly.

'Come on!' Val snapped. 'Give my back a rub. You're not in the nick now.'

With a faint sigh Christy raised his arms to the back of Val's neck. His face was a mask of embarrassment as he pressed down with his thumbs.

'Ah,' Val breathed, closing his eyes, 'that's terrific. You've a great pair of hands, Christy.'

The door to the sauna opened in a billow of steam, and the club's chief instructor – a smooth-faced young man with a torso bursting out of his sleeveless vest – pushed through, chatting briskly to a new customer. Christy's hands instantly dropped from Val's shoulders.

'Hey.' Val turned to him. 'What's the matter?'

Christy's face was down, looking away, colouring. 'Come on,' he murmured.

Val glanced at the newcomers, and then burst out laughing. Good old Christy, straight as the barrel of a sawn-off shotgun! Shaking his head, he turned back to the wall mirror and resumed combing his hair.

'And we've private sauna suites too,' the chief instructor was saying. 'This is the changing room – my name's Tony, by the way.' His hand shot out, perfectly horizontal. The new customer took it without looking.

'Peter,' he said flatly. He was in his early twenties, leather-jacketed, good-looking; he seemed fascinated by the two men standing at the opposite end of the room. *Another conquest for Val*, Tony thought idly. He said, 'Pleased to meet you, Peter. Come on down to the office.'

Mark followed the man through a second door and down the staircase beyond. He felt hard, elated, armoured by cold purpose. He was going to get the bastard. He didn't know how or when, but he was close and it would be soon. Then he would make amends – for every pain, every insult, every betrayal Danny had ever suffered.

He found himself in a small, cluttered office beside the

club entrance. The chief instructor handed him an application form and a biro. 'We've all the equipment,' he was saying, 'bench press, lateral raisers, and military stances – ' He nodded towards the form. 'That's for a year's full membership.'

Stony-faced, Mark began writing, 'Peter', when voices in the corridor outside distracted him. Val appeared through a sliding glass window opening on to the corridor. He rapped on the glass. 'See you Tony!' Nodding briefly, Christy followed him outside.

'He's here every day,' the instructor explained. 'Loves the place.'

Mark gazed after the two men. Threads were coming together, connections being made. He had taught himself to solve impossible problems step by step, move by move – he'd do the same again, but faster now, lightly, thinking on his feet, because men like Bourke and McGuigan would only allow him one opportunity, one chance to put things right.

'Do you not have an address?'

Mark looked blankly at the chief instructor, and then snapped back to the present. He glanced back at the form in front of him. The second man would have been Christy, Christy O'Connor, Val's resident heavy. The man with the golden shotgun. Christy had been Danny's route to Val.

Mark began writing quickly – an address in Mountjoy Square. Danny's last bedsit.

Chapter 18

The quays were quiet as Mark turned by the Custom House and drew into the kerb opposite a narrow, unlit alleyway. It was just before eleven, too early for the streets to fill from emptying pubs; a mild drizzle deterred lingering passers-by.

Mark had put on his new leathers, light-swallowing black from helmet to steel-capped boots. He propped the Suzuki, glanced up and down the street, and melted into the darkness of the alley. The elderly office building which housed D-Day Couriers had seemed without light from the front. The rear looked no different to Mark. A caretaker's flat on the top floor had been empty for months. It was the main reason why the rear fire door did not close the last inch, jammed by boxed rubbish which tenants had been too lazy to carry to the street. Curling his gloved fingers around the edge, Mark wrenched at the door. It gave with a loud clatter; broken files sloughed out in a gentle avalanche.

Mark waited, holding his breath, then lifted his head to the dark canyon of brick that surrounded him. Not a light. Not a sound.

He climbed through the open doorway, barely trusting his weight to the stacked waste inside. The corridor beyond led straight to the stairs rising from the street door.

He reached the second floor without light. Then, pulling a pencil torch and a filed screwdriver from his jacket pocket, he went to work on the door of D-Day Couriers. The lock was ridiculously, almost suspiciously easy. Slipping inside, he closed the door again and moved directly to Carol's desk. He took two packets from a drawer and four address labels from the desk top. Then he turned to the filing cabinet against the wall.

In the torchlight the lock at the top right of the cabinet looked complicated; too small for the crude force of his screwdriver. Mark frowned. He had come here for evidence, records, accounts, anything to link Bourke and D-Day; a few packets and labels hardly justified the risk.

He couldn't leave it now. He pushed the tip of the screwdriver into the lock, feeling for a purchase, but, no matter what angle he tried, the metal shaft was too thick. Angrily he slapped the top drawer. To his astonishment it clicked and rolled forward. The damn thing wasn't even locked!

He yanked it fully open. Two pencils rolled across the empty bottom. He pulled out the second drawer, the third, the fourth – half a dozen unused notepads, three biros, a Mars bar.

No records, no accounts, nothing – not even the daily roster sheets. Carol had to bring them in every day, take them home every night. And the couriers were self-employed, paid cash at the end of every week. The firm was a ghost operation, a phantom, little more than a sign on an office door.

Sighing, Mark closed the drawers again, realising how naive he had been. Bourke might act like a thug, but a simple thug didn't own city centre offices, didn't run a string of businesses: the man wasn't going to be caught as easily as this.

Mark paused. He had not been thinking clearly. The D-Day Courier connection had confused him. How had Danny got close to the man? His mind turned in new directions. The visit had not been wasted. He let himself out silently, re-locking the door and retreated downstairs.

'Not a bad day,' said the hair-cutter, snipping steadily.

'No,' Mark grunted.

The cutter had a lean, angular face, too lined and gaunt to fit the bright, loose, overtly fashionable clothes he wore, too craggily masculine to encourage anyone to point out the discrepancy. He seemed to accept Mark's terseness in the spirit of trade; the fewer distractions, the swifter the service. Of course, he could not fail to be aware of his customer's tension through the rigidity of the young man's spine, the stiffness of his skull, the repeated clenching and unclenching of neck muscles. But that was no concern of the cutter. He was not in the business of being a father confessor. Not for the cheapest cut in the house, even if the fellow had asked for him by name. They had hardly exchanged half a dozen words since Mark had entered the shop.

'You were recommended,' said Mark.

'That's nice.' The cutter's glance crossed his momentarily in the wall mirror. Working quickly, fluidly, he moved to the opposite side of Mark's head.

'I want a shooter.'

The cutter's hands froze, his comb still embedded in Mark's dark, cropped locks, his small sharp scissors hanging in mid-air. 'Pardon?'

His eyes fastened on Mark's in the mirror. Their cold wariness brought Mark's fear to the surface. His voice rose an octave. 'I was told to ask for Christy.'

The cutter resumed combing. 'There's no Christy working here.' He moved forward slightly, his back hiding him from the rest of the shop, where a girl cutter worked on a second customer. The razor tip of his scissors pressed into Mark's neck. 'But there's a lot of fuzz back here,' he hissed. 'You know what I mean?'

The fear jumped into Mark's eyes; sucking in breath, he strained backwards, away from the sharp steel. 'I told you! I'm looking for a shooter.'

'Do I know you?'

He felt a vein pulse against the scissor's edge; the pressure increased.

'I've got a chick – working in a bank – ' It was his last card: one he had not wanted to play. He stared at the cutter's reflection, willing him to respond, but the man's eyes were down, watching the taut veins of his neck.

'Where are you from?'

Mark swallowed, and felt his flesh puncture. 'I'm strung out – right!'

For long seconds the pressure was the same, then, slowly, it relaxed. The scissors retreated, leaving a small, bright bead of red. The cutter's eyes lifted to Mark's. They were still cold, but triumphant, relishing the moment of supremacy.

Mark breathed in, not daring to show relief. Smiling, the cutter began to fluff Mark's hair from the back, rougher than he had been only moments before. 'Only nice clean jobs,' the cutter told him. 'Good cuts.' His smile widened at his choice of words.

Mark nodded.

'OK.' The cutter whisked the towel from Mark's shoulders, used it to brush the loose hair from his neck. 'Call back tomorrow.'

He turned, lifting Mark's jacket from a rack and holding it out to him. Mark climbed out of the chair, and took it. He followed the man to the cash desk.

'That'll be six pounds fifty,' the cutter said. Mark gave him a ten-pound note.

'Thanks for the tip, sir. That's extremely generous of you.'

Mark's face fell as the register slammed shut on the note. The cutter's smile was fixed, wolfish, inviting protest. When Mark said nothing, he picked up a tissue from beneath the desk. 'I'd bring a few more of those notes with you,' he said. 'Say about ten. Shooters come expensive.' He handed over the tissue, smiling again. 'For your neck. Don't want to go bleeding in the street, do we?'

Snatching it, Mark turned and left. Outside he walked quickly, as fast as his beating heart.

'I met Christy through Alfie,' Danny had told him. *'Alfie runs his own salon – place off Aungier Street – he's clean but he enjoys a bit of excitement – that's why Christy likes him. They're mates from way back.'*

He walked faster, his adrenalin fear fading, a colder, darker dread taking hold. I am committed now. No more game playing. No more posing. No going back.

'These guys are animals, Mark. Fucking animals!'

Animals die too, Danny. Animals can be put down. Some have to be.

Chapter 19

Colette had seen Danny in his coffin, his hair brushed and neat, his face waxy smooth, wiped clean of pain, and strain and fear; closed, even his lost eye had looked whole again. He had not looked real. A plaster image, perhaps, to bolster his mother's tattered illusions, but it had not been the Danny Colette had known. Not the Danny who had cried so often on her shoulder; not the Danny whose bloodied needles she had pushed from sight beneath her mattress; not the Danny whose desperate needs had trapped her and drained her just as much as they had him. She had been with him through the worst of his short life; she could hardly close her eyes to his death, whatever its manner, whatever its cause.

The barman had the pub to himself, emptying ashtrays from the tables after early afternoon closing, when she came through the door. He started towards her, ready to point to the clock, then her manner stopped him. She was dressed in a dark business suit, a small silver cross about her neck; her face grave, vulnerable, yet utterly self-contained.

'Excuse me.' She paused by a gate guarding the staircase to the toilet below.

'Yes, love?'

'My brother was the man who died downstairs.'

The barman's face dropped; he had yet to recover from the experience himself. Then compassion overcame his surprise; he stepped forward, lifting his hand.

Colette immediately recoiled, not willing to be comforted,

knowing a touch could shatter her resolution. 'I'd like to go down.'

Made awkward, the barman glanced down the stairwell. 'Well, there's no one down there. If you feel you want to ....'

'Thank you.' She spoke quickly, embarrassed by her need, fumbling at the gate catch. The barman sprang forward, releasing it for her. She slipped through.

'I'll hold on here, then.'

Someone had scrubbed the place recently. Harsh light gleamed off the discoloured tiles; there was a lingering tang of disinfectant. Colette stepped off the stairs beside the door to the only cubicle. A new piece of wood, unpainted yet, had been cut in at the height of the lock.

Fearful, she pushed the door open. The light inside was paler, the disinfectant smell much stronger. But not even the cleaner's efforts could disguise a chipped hand basin, cracked tiles, a length of plastic piping inexpertly repairing the cistern downpipe. It was a cramped, anonymous place. A place without feeling, without resonance.

Colette let out her breath in a slow sigh. Danny had left nothing of himself here. It had simply been his exit point, a way of escape he had been seeking for too long. She turned and walked slowly back up the stairs.

The barman was waiting at the top, clearly anxious that he had not done enough. 'Can I get you a drink – or something?' He gestured helplessly.

'No, I'm fine.'

She took pity on his unease. Moving closer, she put her hand gently on his arm. 'Listen, thank you. Very much.'

He stared at her, not knowing how to respond. Then she turned away and went out of the door.

After work Mark felt too overwrought to go straight home. He could already hear the old silence of the house, and he needed to be tired when he faced it, too eager for sleep to care. Neither did he want to see Colette. Her softness would soften him, and he did not trust himself.

Step by step. Brick by brick. Build walls not even a shotgun blast could penetrate. Or the broken edge of a light bulb.

He saw Val Bourke's face, the dark, overhanging hair, the heavy beak of the nose, the dark glitter of the eyes. Then it swelled and shattered like a ripe fruit dropping on hard ground – blood and bone and brain – bursting explosively.

Would a shooter do that? Or would it be a neat, clean, red-rimmed hole straight through the forehead? He knew which he preferred.

He pulled the throttle back hard, feeling the bike leap under him, burning up the miles along the road to the airport, burning off the tension that threatened to eat him live.

Night had fallen when he arrived home. He had no idea what time it was. Too exhausted to rifle his pockets for the front door key, he went in through the kitchen door. He could not even be bothered to snap on the light.

The seated figure silhouetted by a neighbour's light made him start. Colette leaned forward, showing a teasing grin. 'Our Danny taught me a trick or two. Always check the back door.'

Mark breathed in, masking the rapid tattoo of his heart by switching on the light. Both blinked in the sudden glare.

'Very nice,' he said.

'For a girl who works in a bank.' Colette chuckled. She was sitting at the kitchen table, her back to the dresser. She lifted up a bottle of wine.

'I'll get glasses,' Mark said.

He went straight past her. A dresser drawer was half open, D-Day courier packets visible inside. He pushed it shut with his body, stretching up to reach two glasses off a high shelf. Perhaps it had been dark when she arrived. She might not have glanced in the drawer.

'What's up?' The concern was evident in her voice. He realised he should have kissed her a moment ago, shared her joke; he realised too that he was quite unable to maintain any sort of veneer. The relationship didn't work like that.

He turned, setting the glasses down on the table. 'Nothing,' he said. 'I just don't feel too good.'

He could not meet her gaze. Sighing, he leaned back against the dresser. 'I'm thinking of selling the house,' he said. 'I'm thinking of leaving.'

He had not planned the decision, had not even thought of it clearly before he spoke. But, saying it, its inevitability became obvious to him. The one-way path he had set upon left no other choice.

The momentousness of the decision showed instantly in Colette's look of shock. 'When?' she asked softly.

'As soon as possible. I want you to come with me.'

There was real distress in Colette's face. She was already shaking her head. 'No. I'm not ready yet, Mark. Not for a decision like that.'

Mark felt frustration rise in him; this was why he had not wanted to see her tonight. He had to convince her immediately. 'Look,' he said, dropping to her side, 'we can just go.'

'No!' Her tone was sharp. 'Not yet. God, it's not as simple as that.'

'It can be.'

'I just want everything to be normal, Mark, just for a while. Just back to normal. I need that.'

He sighed; he needed things clear at her end – couldn't she see that?

Her hand rose to his cheek. 'Look, it's not that I don't

want to.' He dropped his head. 'I just need time.'

He looked back at her, swallowing his disappointment. 'Yeah. OK.'

There was moisture in her eyes. The burden was his – he should have realised that. It couldn't be any other way. Later he would try again; later she would understand. His look softened. He smiled faintly, touching her hand.

Chapter 20

During his lunch break the following day Mark rode home, making two calls en route, the first at his bank to cash a large cheque, the second at a supermarket to buy three packets of the same brand of breakfast cereal. On his kitchen table he opened all three, emptied the contents into bowls and removed the free gift each packet contained – a selection of brightly coloured transfers depicting comic book super-heroes.

Carefully he picked out each transfer predominantly coloured blue. Then he shrugged off his jacket, took the first transfer – it featured Batman – moistened it under the tap and smeared it against his left wrist. He peeled back the transfer, studying the result. It looked like a black smudge. Frowning, he reached out and tore off a strip of kitchen roll, dampened it and dabbed it lightly over the stain. The colour began to lighten. In a moment it took on the pale-blue likeness of a bruise.

Happier, he stretched out his forearm, turned it palm upwards and bunched his fist. He slapped the flesh just below the elbow several times, clenching and unclenching his fingers, so that the veins rose. The fake bruise was in the right position – along the line of the veins. At a casual glance it could pass for needle tracks. He hoped even that might not be necessary.

Breathing in, he went back for another transfer. Then, carefully, he began to work his way down the length of his forearm.

He was at the hairdressing salon just after three – the same time as the previous day. Parking the bike in a neighbouring street, he locked his helmet to the side of the frame, pushed his radiophone inside and jammed his D-Day vest on top of it.

The shop was busy. Alfie was in tight jeans today, with a neat, colourful tie. He acknowledged Mark with a curt nod, motioning him to a chair for waiting customers.

Twenty minutes later Mark was still sitting there. He had wangled a long delivery, out to Dun Laoghaire, but every passing moment stretched his excuse. Carol could well be calling him already. It was her style to arrange a pick-up on the return route. He could feel the prickle of sweat beneath the arms of his tee-shirt, and worried that the dampness would ruin his fake bruises.

He flicked for the tenth time through the same magazine, still seeing nothing, when he felt Alfie suddenly touch his shoulder. As he glanced up, the man lifted his head to the window. Outside a blue BMW had drawn up by the kerb. The BMW Mark had followed to the Body Club. Christy was visible inside.

Heart thumping, Mark hurried to the front passenger door. As he slipped inside, Christy engaged the clutch and the car shot away, throwing him back into the seat. 'OK, where's the stroke?'

Mark stared at him. He had on the same jacket he had been wearing in the gym. There, he had been dwarfed by Val, despite looming over the older man. Now he was very definitely in charge.

'What?'

Christy stamped on the brake. The car squealed to a dead stop. Mark flung up an arm to prevent himself smashing into the dashboard. 'Get out then.' Christy's gaze was hard.

'OK. OK.' Mark swallowed. 'It's in Dame Street. National General Bank.'

110

He took a deep, ragged breath as Christy moved off again. The man relaxed, a glint coming to his eye. He was enjoying himself.

'This isn't granny bashing – get that straight in your head.' He glanced meaningfully at Mark. 'Or sticking your fingers in the till.'

Mark nodded.

'All you know is the chick, right? What is she?'

'A teller,' Mark said.

'On the counter?'

'Yeah.'

Christy seemed pleased. 'OK. Let's go and have a butchers.'

They turned into Aungier Street, followed the traffic flow into Dame Street and pulled off College Green on to the quiet cobbles bordering the bank's tree-shaded eighteenth-century facade. Christy braked and cut the engine. He pointed to the glove compartment. 'You can drop a ton in there for starters.'

Mark reached into his jacket pocket and pulled out a roll of notes. As he pushed it into the glove compartment, Christy's hand shot out suddenly, gripping his wrist and wrenching it over.

Perspiration had blurred Mark's 'bruises', spreading their effect even wider. He held his breath as Christy bent close. 'Jesus.' Christy's face rose again, his expression one of amused disgust. He tossed Mark's hand back at him.

'Alfie's a psycho,' he said. 'He'd cut your balls off with those scissors of his. Remember that.'

Mark blinked, pulling his jacket sleeve back over his arm. He was hardly likely to forget.

Christy looked back at the bank, appraising it with a professional eye. The roadway was quiet, leaving a clear run. Nothing to stop you once you'd made the door. *If* you made it. Then he realised that the place could only have closed a few moments ago, yet no one had stirred from inside.

'Wages day?' he asked.

Mark nodded.

Christy smiled, pleased with himself. He gazed at Mark for a long minute, holding his eyes, making up his mind. 'Yeah. OK,' he decided at last. 'This is the score. Alfie fixes the drop, you get two cartridges – twenty-four hours, then you pay half the take the newspapers print.'

'*Half* the take?'

Christy's look was suddenly cold. 'Look, who are you? You're nobody! I'm risking a good shooter on you.'

Mark's mouth opened, then a movement at the bank entrance caught his eye. Two young women were leaving. His heart lurched. One of them was Colette.

'OK,' Mark said quickly.

Seeing the reaction, Christy turned. Colette waved goodbye to the second girl and moved towards the car. Horrified, Mark sank back into his seat. Then she turned off the pavement between two parked cars and cut away to the left.

Mark breathed in and straightened. Christy was watching him, enjoying the little drama. His glance took in Colette's retreating back, dropped to her legs. He chuckled, appreciatively.

'I can do it myself . . . .'

'I said OK!' There was a sheen of sweat on Mark's forehead, desperation in his eyes.

'Jesus. All you junkies are the same.' Christy shook his head sadly. Did no one rob for pleasure any more? Did every tear-away in Dublin get his kicks from the point of a needle? God, in a few years' time his own daughter would be this guy's age. He was beginning to feel like a dinosaur. He nodded at the door. 'Go on. Talk to Alfie.'

Mark got out of the car. As he pushed the door shut,

Christy suddenly leaned across, calling, 'Hey, hey, hey . . . .'

Mark bent to the open passenger window. 'Yeah?'

'What do you call a junkie in a suit?' Christy was grinning from ear to ear. Mark stared at him, totally confused. 'What?' 'The accused!'

Roaring with laughter, Christy twisted the ignition key and pulled away. Mark watched him go, relief and fear mingling so violently he felt his gorge rise. His whole body was trembling; he was bathed in sweat. It was a full minute before the sickness passed. Then he turned and started back for his bike, breaking into a run as he went.

That night he cleared his kitchen table, and methodically gathered together on its top one two-pound packet of glucose, another of flour, a mixing bowl, a dessert spoon, a small weighing balance, a D-day courier packet and several small, plastic, re-sealable envelopes. Then he sat, poured quantities of glucose and flour into the bowl, and mixed them thoroughly with the spoon. Next he took a spoonful of the mixture and tipped it carefully into a plastic envelope. He hooked the envelope on the weighing balance and slowly raised it. The colour and texture looked right, but it was several grammes too light.

His hand shook and the envelope dropped, spilling white powder explosively across the table top. He took a deep breath, closing his eyes while he breathed out slowly. Then he opened them again, brushed the loose powder aside and began to re-fill the envelope.

There had been five envelopes in the delivery he had intercepted. Other packets had been about the same weight. No point in taking chances. He'd fill seven, for luck.

Chapter 21

At eleven thirty the next morning Mark found a call box and rang Alfie's salon. When the man realised who it was his public voice collapsed into a savage hiss. 'Where the bloody hell have you been?'

'I've got a job.'

'What the fuck is a junkie doing with a job!' He paused, modulating his anger. 'Listen. I'll only say it once. It's under an old fridge door, arches off Seville Terrace, third one along.'

'I'll pick it up at lunchtime.'

'It'll be there for another half hour!'

'But ...'

The line went dead.

He was there in ten minutes. A dim, dank place, beneath an elderly railway viaduct, water dripping from the brickwork. Waste ground to one side, a wall to the other.

Propping the bike, he saw so much rubbish he began to panic. But the fridge door was there, half hidden by sacking and rotting cardboard. He looked in every direction before turning it over with the tip of his boot. Bricks had been removed to make a narrow cache. A long bundle, wrapped tightly in a black plastic bag, filled the space.

Mark bent and picked it up. He pulled off the plastic. The weapon was old, well-used, its double barrel – no more than twelve inches long – blackened, its stock replaced by a smooth, wooden grip. Mark broke it, and saw two cartridges in the breach. He snapped it shut again.

Loosening his courier vest, he unzipped his jacket, slipped the gun inside, then zipped up again.

He took another swift look up and down the arches. No one in sight. Then he allowed himself the luxury of a sigh. Sweet Jesus, he was going to have to carry the damn thing around half the day.

His radiophone barked into life. 'Three-two-four, Mark! Three-two-four, Mark!'

He got back on his bike, and thumbed the return button. 'On my way back, Carol. Some traffic problems.'

'Don't bother. There's a call from Value Video. Usual run. OK?'

His heart stopped. The stolen packet – carefully weighed – bulged against his chest. He had hoped for a breather, a day at least to collect his senses, to regain some equilibrium.

'Did you get that, Mark?'

'OK, Carol. No problem.' He sounded almost normal. His heart had started again; it was beginning to flutter wildly, a nervous trill.

The lift closed behind him. Visor down, he crossed the corridor to the video company's outer door. For the first time he was not greeted by the clatter of typing.

The typist's office was empty. He hesitated. Nothing was going quite as he had planned; everything was happening too quickly.

He heard a rustle of paper from the inner office. The door was ajar. Whoever was inside would have heard him enter. He could not retreat now. He knocked on the door and pushed it open.

Val lounged in the chair behind his desk, leafing through a stapled product list. He wore a new, light-coloured suit, a dark, polo-necked shirt, high against his throat. He looked up, smiling amiably. 'How's it going?'

Mark stepped forward into the room, his gaze rivetted by Val. 'Collection,' he said.

Val nodded, reached down to a drawer, pulled it open and drew out a small brown packet. It looked exactly the same as all the others. He tossed it across the desk.

Mark leaned forward to pick it up, putting his receipt pad in its place. The shotgun pushed against his armpit. His eyes fell, but the bulk of his courier vest hid the unnatural bulge. He glanced up at Val, blinking as sweat blurred his vision. The man was casually scribbling his signature, not even looking at him.

I could do it now, Mark thought. *Yank it from the jacket, cock, fire. Would the force of both barrels blast him through the window? Or would his face simply dissolve?*

Val's eyes lifted, narrowed fractionally at the intensity of Mark's gaze. Shaken, Mark nodded quickly at the picture window behind Val's head. 'Nice view.'

Val grunted softly, amused. There was something familiar about the lad. Had he seen him before, somewhere outside the office? He never usually forgot a pretty face. He handed back the receipt pad. 'It gets better the higher up you go,' he purred, and his smile spread softly, his eyes glittering.

Mark nodded. 'Sure.' He turned quickly, going while he could, feeling the man's gaze on his back.

He hurried to the bike, his heart hammering inside his chest. There was no need for haste. It would only matter on the return journey, but he could not slow himself. The quicker things happened, the less chance for mistakes. He did not trust events; they slewed away from him, pursuing their own ends.

Foolishly, unnecessarily, he swapped the packets as he rode, pushing the genuine one inside his jacket, against his chest, tucking his faked version just inside his courier vest. He felt the shotgun slip, and slapped a hand against his midriff, wobbling dangerously. A car on his tail hooted sharply. Straightening on the saddle, he increased his speed.

It was like a needle-less high. But a high without pleasure, sharpening not dulling the senses. The adrenalin coursing through his veins gave him new insights. The video editor, he realised, moved at the same rhythm as the cuts he made – each staccato movement was a fresh angle, changing on the beat of the music. Today the monitors showed seascapes, a band playing along cliff edges or beside spray-enshrouded rocks.

Mark dropped the fake packet on the desk beside him. The editor reached to one side and lifted an identical envelope. 'Cheers. There's the bread.'

Mark bent to take it, astonished by his openness. Did the man assume he was part of the network, or did he just not care? As he straightened, the editor suddenly swivelled in his chair, shooting out a hand and grasping the front of Mark's vest. Mark froze. The man's knuckles were hard against the barrel of the shotgun.

It was the first time the editor had looked him in the face. His eyes were glassy, barely focussed; reflected images of sea and sky danced in them. 'Stay on top, man!' he hissed. His mouth cracked in a brief conspiratorial grin. Then, chuckling, he turned back to the screens.

Breathing in, Mark rushed to the stairs.

His heart boomed now like a bell, slow and sonorous, measuring each moment. In Abbey Street the traffic piled suddenly, filling the smallest gap, within yards of a call box. Swearing, Mark bumped the kerb and rode the last few feet along the pavement. He propped his bike, flung open the kiosk door and snatched off his helmet, dialling immediately.

'Hello,' he snapped. 'I want to speak to Detective Inspector McGuigan. No,' he shook his head violently. 'No

118

name – tell him it's about Val Bourke. Hurry!'

He held on, staring at the traffic, smacking the side of the telephone with his bunched fist.

McGuigan's slow drawl filled the earpiece. 'McGuigan here. Who is this?'

'Val Bourke is about to get a special delivery,' Mark snapped. 'Top grade stuff.' He gave the address. 'You got ten minutes.' He slammed down the receiver, and ran to his bike.

The editor was rewinding his tapes. Grey dots jostled on the banked monitors. In the pale, flickering light he reached for the courier packet, peeled it open and shook out a plastic envelope. Smiling, he cracked the seal, wet a fingertip and dipped it into the white powder inside. He tasted it. His smile faded. With an expression of disgust, he spat. Frowning, he reached for the telephone.

Mark came through the glass doors of the office building at speed, aiming for the lift. Ten minutes. If McGuigan was as keen as he thought he'd make it in five.

He had thumped the call button three times before he realised the lift was not going to come. It sank from the sixth floor, stopped and rose again. He rushed to a staircase that he had seen rising beside the entrance. Half a dozen steps up he saw that it only led to a mezzanine. He ran back to the lift, turned a corner and found a broad stairwell climbing through the centre of the building. He went up two steps at a time, bumping into a man on the first landing, scattering an apology behind him.

The typist's office was still unoccupied. Swallowing his gasps, he heard Val's voice through the open door of his office. 'I *told* you. It's good stuff – it's the best in Dublin.' His eyes jerked up as Mark appeared in the doorway. He was still at his desk, a telephone in his hand. Without another word, he replaced the receiver.

'Return package,' Mark announced, stepping forward, holding it out.

'On the desk.' The amiability had gone, the casualness. Val was like a coiled snake, his gaze heavy with violence.

Mark set down the unlabelled packet, his receipt pad. Slowly Val leaned forward, picked up a pen, scribbled his signature. His eyes rose again to Mark's, boring into them. 'How's Carol?'

Mark blinked, giving him nothing, keeping his mind blank. 'She's OK.'

With a sharp flick of his wrist, Val propelled the receipt pad across the desk.

Mark stooped to retrieve it. As he rose, he saw the intensity of Val's gaze had not wavered.

He did not think he would be allowed to reach the door. He did not think he would be allowed to reach the corridor. He did not breath again until he was descending the stairs.

Chapter 22

'*Somebody* is screwing you, Val.'

Val sat quietly, the video editor's phone call still ringing in his ears. He had received the latest shipment early this morning, already divided into envelopes. Mary had had her delivery first thing. He'd have heard long before now if there was any problem.

But he'd only checked two envelopes from the whole shipment, at random. It had become his established practice. Everything had been fine for weeks. No one would risk doctoring *half* a shipment – surely?

He sighed and climbed to his feet, staring out across the city. The stuff had only been out of his hands once since it had arrived. When the courier had picked it up from here . . . . If the little sod was working a fast one he'd be a cripple by teatime.

Val's eyes dipped from the skyline to the street directly below. A car skidded to a halt against the opposite kerb. The driver's door flew open and a man in a dark brown overcoat jumped out. Val recognised McGuigan.

'*Fuck!*' Swinging round, he snatched the return packet off his desk, ripping it open. Five envelopes of white powder spilled on to the desk top. Bundling them together, he ran into the toilet, spinning both taps on the washbasin. As the water flowed, he began tearing the envelopes open, flushing away the contents. He panted as he worked, his heart bumping.

That little *bastard* – that little *gobshite*. A stroke like this was worth more than a knee-capping. Christ, he'd blind the shit for this, he'd rip his fucking face off!

Fumbling in his pocket, Val pulled out a cigarette lighter, held the emptied envelopes over the toilet bowl and thumbed the lighter beneath them. He winced as the plastic flared, scorching his fingers.

The kid was dead meat. The kid was history . . . .

Mark hung back in the shadow of the stairwell as McGuigan entered the entrance foyer at a run. Casting a swift glance at the companies listed on the wall, the detective made straight for the stairs. His face was hard-set, anxious.

As soon as he had disappeared round the first landing, Mark emerged, crossed the foyer and left the building. His bike was parked immediately outside. He climbed aboard, started it up and swung across the road in an abrupt U-turn, braking beside McGuigan's unmarked car. Pulling the genuine return packet from his vest, he bent, opened the driver's door and jammed the packet beneath the driver's seat. He slammed the door again, just as a Garda car, lights flashing, siren wailing, screamed to a halt across the road. Three men, two uniformed, one not, got out and ran into the building.

Mark pulled away. He rode back to the telephone kiosk he had used before, parked and, less frantic now, dialled the Garda. 'Internal Investigation, please. No, no name. I'll ring off if you don't put me through.'

There was a pause. Another phone was picked up.

'Internal Investigation? McGuigan's been doing favours. Have a look in his car today.'

He put down the receiver, and held it a long moment, letting the air slowly fill his lungs. For the first time in what seemed like years he felt an inkling of relief.

Then he straightened. The thing was done. Now let the animals tear themselves to pieces.

122

'Jesus, McGuigan!' Val greeted him with a half smile. 'Do you never stop?'

He was slumped back in his chair, his feet up on the desk. But McGuigan's eyes saw the flush in his cheeks, the sheen of perspiration on his forehead. The man stank of panic. The detective had struck lucky.

Breathless himself, he glanced appreciatively round the office. 'New premises, Val?'

'Yeah!' Val swung his legs down and hunched forward, abandoning all efforts at affability. 'I'm expanding the business. I'm looking into the feasibility of opening somewhere else.'

McGuigan nodded and picked up an unlabelled cassette from the desk top. 'Porno's always good business, you know, Val,' he remarked.

Footsteps thudded in the outer office. Dunne, bright-eyed, appeared in the doorway with two uniformed Garda.

Val sucked in breath. 'You're harassing me, McGuigan!' he snapped.

McGuigan turned to the newcomers. 'Tear this place apart,' he said easily, and looked back at Val with a faint smile. 'Tear it to bits.'

'Oh, that's great! Go on – wreck it!' Visibly rattled, Val sprang to his feet, backing against the picture window as the officers surged into the room. Display material winnowed to the floor. Filing cabinets thumped open. Val was breathing fast, eyes wide. 'Val's Video!' he cried, throwing up his hands. 'What do you think?'

McGuigan let the cassette he was holding drop on to the desk top. 'You're slipping up, Val,' he said. 'I thought you were a better rat catcher.'

Behind him, Dunne turned a fierce smile on Val as his hand stretched out, shunting a whole stack of videos off a cabinet top.

Val exploded, stabbing a finger at the pair. 'You know

what! I'm putting in a complaint about you, McGuigan!'

Untroubled, McGuigan gave him a look of mock puzzlement. 'People just keep telling me things,' he said. 'Don't you find that curious, Val?'

Val glared back at him, his fists clenching and unclenching. *Dead meat*, he thought. *Dead meat.*

Chapter 23

Carol did not like Christy; she never had on any of the half dozen occasions their paths had crossed. He was a swaggerer, an adolescent bully-boy who thought macho brashness and an easy smile were the ticket to any woman's bedroom. She couldn't understand why Val bothered with him. When he appeared at D-Day's office she made no effort to hide her opinion. She watched his grin fade under her glare.

'The lad who did the warehouse run. Twelve o'clock today,' he said, settling on the front of her desk, and turning his back to her. 'Just get out his address.'

His smile returned as he took in the only other occupant of the room. Sharon leaned against the window sill, lifting her eyebrows, as Christy's approving gaze swept her from head to foot and back again.

He got up, moving across towards her and glancing out the window. 'He's been a bold boy,' he confided.

'Oh.' Sharon tccched softly.

Carol got up from her desk. 'Forty two, Marino Park Drive,' she said.

'Just write it down, love,' Christy told her, still smiling at the blonde girl.

'Why?' Carol snapped. 'Can you read?'

Now Christy looked at her. He began to chuckle softly. Any woman who loathed him so obviously had to have some interest. He asked Sharon, 'Nice to work for, is she?'

Sharon shrugged. 'Nicer than some.' Her gaze slid away from his, no longer encouraging him. Grunting, Christy returned to the desk, taking a slip of paper from Carol.

He lavished a parting smile on Sharon. 'Be good.'

'Be careful,' she replied.

As the door shut on him, Carol went to the window. Frowning, she looked down into the street. Val's BMW was parked against the opposite kerb.

'Got him!' beamed Christy, leaning in through the passenger window and flicking Carol's note triumphantly between his fingers.

Val glanced at him coldly. His mood had not improved in the previous two hours. McGuigan's men had taken him at his word. The office was a wreck; even the hessian had been ripped from the walls.

'Right,' he snapped. 'Break his legs, then find out what he wants.'

Christy laughed easily. 'He's only freelancing, isn't he?'

'He's got a funny way of freelancing.' Val's face was dark. 'He sent the smack back!'

'I thought the trade went OK,' Christy said, puzzled.

'Yeah, so did I – so it seemed – these people can be funny.' Val stabbed a finger at him, his anger barely contained. 'Now you get out of here, and you find him!' He turned back to the windscreen, clutching at the steering wheel.

Christy paused, then he shrugged and sauntered off.

Sighing, Val reached for the ignition. As he turned it, Carol appeared suddenly on the pavement opposite. 'Val!' she called. 'Wait.'

He paused as she tottered across the street, unsteady on over-high heels, her jacket flapping. Breathless, she ducked her head into his window. 'Val, I'm sorry.'

He nodded, not looking at her. She was fat and sweaty and too close. 'What happened?' he snapped.

'There was something funny,' she gasped. 'I just couldn't

say – I don't know . . . .' To his utter astonishment tears welled into her eyes; her head dropped. 'I'm sorry I let you down!'

Val looked at her. He'd never dreamed she felt so personally involved. He had only given her the job because he owed a favour to a relative of hers. Until now she'd struck him as something of a hard-faced cow. He stretched out his hand and put it lightly over hers. Her head lifted.

'It's alright.' He smiled. 'Don't worry about it. OK?'

She nodded, sighing, only partially mollified.

He pulled back his hand, slipped into gear and shot away. *Christ*, he thought. *If I had a little more loyalty like that I wouldn't be in this shit.*

Drawing herself up, Carol plunged her hands into her jacket pockets and went back across the road. From the nearest corner Mark watched her, sinking back out of sight as she drew near. He let his helmeted head fall back against the wall, his brain whirring.

What was Val doing *here*? No one got out on bail this quickly, not with the quantity of smack McGuigan should have uncovered. Why hadn't he been arrested? Why *wasn't* he in custody?

He closed his eyes, and sighed. None of it made any sense. Nothing was happening the way he'd planned. All he knew was that Bourke would now be looking for him, and a man who maimed for one quiet chat with a detective wouldn't give up until he was found.

'What's that?' asked McGuigan.

The inspector from Internal Investigation turned the brown courier packet over in his hand. 'You tell me,' he said. He was tall and fortyish with a thick ginger moustache, a schoolmasterly manner. A manner members of his department tended to acquire quickly.

He rose from the front seat of McGuigan's car, squeezing the packet open so that McGuigan could see the notes inside. 'There's the best part of fifteen thousand pounds here,' he said.

McGuigan was frowning. 'Somebody is trying to set me up.'

'I hope so.'

They began to walk across the drug squad carpark towards a car where a young Garda stood.

'Is it Bourke?' asked the inspector.

'I don't know,' said McGuigan. 'Val was a worried man when I arrived.'

'Val?' The inspector paused. 'That's a bit familiar, isn't it?'

McGuigan had drawn ahead. He turned to glare at the man. 'Don't cheapen yourself!'

The inspector was unabashed. He moved closer. 'Just be careful you don't either,' he warned. 'You're losing touch, McGuigan.'

'Is that all?' the older man snapped, deeply angry.

'For the time being, yes.' The inspector handed the courier packet to the waiting Garda. 'Get that counted properly and booked in,' he told him. With a final glance at McGuigan he walked away.

John Patrick stood in silence a moment, swallowing his temper. First Danny, now this. It was too crude for Bourke – too crude, in itself, to stick. But after the Adams fiasco, if there were enough anti-McGuigan voices in the force, it might tip the balance for early retirement. How the Dunnes of this world would love that!

And, perhaps, too, he might deserve it. But not yet. Lord, not quite yet!

Chapter 24

He rode until it got dark, up to Howth, back across the northern suburbs to Phoenix Park, down into the city again. He thought of taking the bike to Dun Laoghaire and jumping the first ferry. He thought of going north. He could not stay; he could not leave, not without Colette. He could not make his brain work any more!

Only one thing made sense. He had ruined his life, perhaps even thrown it away. For nothing.

He needed to touch ground. He needed something, someone he could still trust. He needed to talk. He stopped at a call box in Abbey Street and rang Colette's house.

Her mother answered. 'Isn't she with you, Mark?'

'I'm sorry . . . .'

'Well, she only left a few minutes ago. I'll expect she'll be along soon.'

'Oh I see. Yes, thanks, Mrs Adams.'

A knot tightened in his stomach as he put down the receiver. Val would have his address from Carol. He would be watching the house. Sweet Jesus, Colette might be there already.

Mark picked up his helmet and ran to his bike.

Christy's buttocks were beginning to ache. He had been perched here on the stairs, in the dark, for over an hour. Occasionally the headlamps of a passing car would brighten the frosted glass in the front door below him, scattering saucers of light about the narrow hall. But not very often. It was a hell of a dull neighbourhood.

He took turns stretching each leg, shifting the position of the pump action shotgun that straddled his knees. Was this going to be an all-nighter?

The courier was obviously off his head, or so bloody thick he didn't know what he was doing. Whatever he was, Christy would make it quick. One quick blast, and he was off. Now he was out of that hellhole of a flat, he had a warm bed to share at night. Let Val do his own bloody interrogations.

High heels clicked on the pavement outside. As they paused, Christy looked up, tensing. A gate clattered; the footsteps resumed, approaching the front door.

Grasping the shotgun, Christy got to his feet. A figure appeared behind the frosted glass, small, feminine. He saw a hand rise. The door bell rang, shatteringly, the sound filling the hall.

Training the gun on the door, Christy backed quietly up the stairs. As he moved across the landing to the main bedroom, the bell rang again. The bedroom curtains were open. Christy squeezed against one side of the window, and squinted down through the nets.

A girl moved back from the front door, glancing up at the front of the house. She wore slacks with a man's shirt hanging over the waist band, a short jacket in some kind of shiny plastic. Christy frowned. He'd seen that face before, only recently. Outside the National General Bank. The junkie's girlfriend?

She turned and walked across the front lawn, vanishing around the side of the house. Worried, Christy moved back from the window. This was starting to feel wrong. He didn't like coincidences. He didn't like witnesses. He sank back against the wall, tightening his grip on the shotgun. Downstairs a door opened and shut.

Colette switched on the kitchen light, blinking in the neon

130

glare. She liked the idea that Mark still left his back door unlocked. Just for her? Perhaps there was something psychological about it. He had been so uptight the last time they had been together. It was almost as if he was taking Danny's death worse than she was, blaming himself. Well, Colette could teach him a thing or two about blame where Danny was concerned; she was an old hand at that unwinnable game. But first Mark needed brightening up; they both did.

She went through into the hallway, and heard a motorbike in the street outside, approaching at speed, slowing and then coughing to a halt. On an impulse she reached back into the kitchen and switched off the light. Grinning, she skipped along the darkened hall and into the living room. There was an old armchair to the right of the door. She kicked off her shoes and climbed on to it. Then she stood with her back to the wall, holding her breath, waiting.

Through the nets Christy watched the motorcyclist prop his bike at the kerbside, then pause, still astride his saddle, and glance up and down the lamp-lit road. *It's in here, buddy boy*, Christy thought. *No surprises for you in the open air.*

Evidently satisfied, the rider dismounted, tugged at his chin strap and pulled off his helmet. He approached the gate, lifting the latch cautiously so that it did not clatter, staring up at the house. The lamplight caught his face.

Christy swore silently. What in *God's* name was the junkie doing here? *He* was the rogue courier? Somebody was playing silly buggers, and Christy – bright boy Christy! – had given the mad bastard a sawn-off.

The house looked dark to Mark. He had not seen Colette on the road, but he had come by the most direct route. She would be using the side streets. He had ridden like the wind.

There was every chance he had beaten her.

Seeing nothing unusual, hearing nothing, he reached the front door, found his key and stepped inside. Ignoring the light switch, he eased the catch down behind him. He placed his helmet on the hall stand, unwound the silk scarf he wore, and then stood silently, absorbing the silence of the house.

'Colette?' he called.

There was something wrong. If he could do nothing right these past few days, he could at least tell when events were slewing out of control again.

He felt a surge of panic. Quashing the urge to turn and run, he unzipped his jacket, pulled out the shotgun and held it before him with both hands, the butt pressed against his stomach. Leathers creaking softly, he moved slowly to the foot of the stairs.

Christy sat on the bedroom floor, back against the window wall, legs outstretched. His shotgun was propped against his midriff, aimed at the top half of the bedroom door. It was an old trick. The man coming in would be looking up. As he caught sight of the body on the floor his eyes would drop into line with the barrel.

Christy licked his lips. He jerked back the gun's pump action, slotting a cartridge into the breach.

Mark heard the click distinctly; his heart jumped. He swung the double barrels up the stairs.

His foot was on the first step, when another sound – softer, but closer – came from the side. The living room. Did that mean two of them? He could not be trapped from behind.

Holding his breath, he turned towards the living-room door, leading with the gun. The twin barrels touched the door panel. He paused, praying silently for help. Then he kicked the door open, throwing himself forward.

'Boo!' Colette shrieked in delight, then in stark terror as Mark swung around the door, shotgun upraised, barrels inches from her face. In the dim light he seemed demoniac, eyes blazing, face a mask of hatred and fear; no one she recognised.

She began to weep, a soft, animal whimper on the edge of a dead faint. As she sank down the wall, the shotgun went with her. 'What's happening?' she whispered.

The tension drained from Mark slowly, still leaving the thunder of blood dinning through his skull. Then his energy was gone. He sagged on to the sofa, the shotgun drooping between his fingers. And the reaction hit him. He lurched forward suddenly, gasping as bile rose in his throat.

Upstairs Christy thumbed a bead of sweat from his eyebrow. What in Christ's name was happening down there? What party games were they playing now?

In a moment the worst of it had gone. Mark's brain slowly cleared. He looked up suddenly at Colette. She was sitting in the armchair, hugging her bunched knees, staring at the carpet.

'How did you get in?' Mark snapped.

She looked up at him blankly.

'How!'

'The back door ...'

Mark shot to his feet, still gripping the shotgun, clutching at Colette's hand. 'Come on.'

'No.' Frightened, she tried to pull away.

'Come *on*!' He yanked her roughly off the chair, dragging her through the door.

In the hall he pushed her behind him, backing towards the front door, gun trained on the stairs. 'Get a helmet,' he snapped. 'Grab your bag.'

She opened the door as he snatched up his own helmet. Terrified, she clung to him as they backed towards the gate, Mark's eyes darting from window to window, swinging the shotgun barrel from side to side. Her high heels caught in a crack and she stumbled.

'Move!' he bellowed. 'Get on the bike.' The rear foot supports were not down. She fumbled with them, protesting.

'Get on the bike!' Mike roared.

As she obeyed him, he pulled on his helmet with one hand, still keeping the gun raised toward the house. Straddling the saddle, he worked his keys from his jacket pocket, pushed them into the ignition, kicked the starter.

The engine took. He jammed the shotgun into his jacket, wrenched on the throttle and the bike leapt away.

From the bedroom window Christy watched them disappear into the night. Thoroughly confused, he turned away and sat down on the end of the bed, his gun propped between his legs. *Now* what the fuck was he supposed to do?

Mark rode towards the city centre, bright lights, cover, anywhere where there were people. It was Colette, collecting her senses first, who gave him his direction. As they stopped for a traffic light in Parnell Street, she tapped his shoulder. 'Duggans,' she cried. 'Go to Duggans.' Mark nodded.

Chapter 25

Val did not like fuck-ups; he did not like losing in excess of twenty grand in the space of a day; most of all he did not like the even tenor of his life radically disturbed. He had pressures no one but he knew about: pressures no one else would believe.

It was nearly ten and there was still no word from Christy. Val could not hold on any longer. He could not count on venting his feelings by proxy.

He left the ruin of his office and collected the BMW from the carpark. He drove across the city centre, almost aimlessly, not thinking of his destination, until he found the car nosing its way off busy streets into a quiet section of the quays. He allowed himself a quiet ripple of surprise and pleasure. He was due for some enjoyment. There had been very little for weeks now. He couldn't really count Danny – that had been business. It wasn't good to work hard all the time.

The car was doing no more than ten miles an hour. Figures appeared in the lights of the headlamps. Youths, lounging at intervals against the quay wall. Some discreet, barely acknowledging his approach, as if waiting on this shadowed stretch of road simply by chance; others posing with exaggerated effeminacy. One, eyes limned by mascara, began to back before the car, bending to the windscreen, his tongue flickering with serpentine speed.

Stupid bugger, thought Val. He disliked show-offs. He preferred partners who were more discreet, more malleable.

He braked. Three youths were held in the car lights. The

one in the middle was small and pale, almost nondescript, no more than seventeen or eighteen; he wore a tee-shirt, tight jeans, a leather jacket. Val beckoned to him.

The youth approached at once, leaning in through the open window of the car.

'How's it going?' Val asked.

The youth shrugged. 'Good.'

Val nodded approvingly. 'That's good.' He ducked his head towards the front passenger seat. 'Get in.'

The boy hurried to obey him.

Colette lifted her head from the hotel washbasin, sweeping her hair back from her dampened face; water and tears mingled on her cheeks. Turning to Mark, she resembled a ghost, a pale, incredulous, enraged ghost. 'What *right* had you? He was *my* brother!'

Mark hung in the bathroom doorway, shotgun in hand, gazing blankly at the floor. 'They *killed* him,' he said, his voice almost a sob.

Colette stared at him, wonderingly. 'I had Danny dragging out of me long enough,' she hissed. 'Why?' He would not look at her. 'Why!' she shrieked.

His head rose abruptly, cracking against the door jamb. 'How do you stop now?' he snapped. 'How?'

Colette shook her head slowly, staring at him. 'You think you're Clint Eastwood – Dirty Harry here with his shotgun.'

Mark sighed, as she fumbled a packet of cigarettes from her slacks pocket, extracted one and lit up. She inhaled deeply, steadying herself.

Abruptly she moved towards the door. 'I'm going to the police.'

'No!' Mark brought up the gun, barring her way.

Colette's eyes lifted from the barrel to Mark's face. They held fear, anger, a disappointment so close to contempt it

136

squeezed at his heart. 'You think you're different from them?' she whispered. '*Do* you?'

He could not bear her look. He was a vacuum swirling with more emotions than he could handle. His self-repair work was gone, smashed beyond recovery. He no longer knew himself. The shotgun dropped to his side. He snapped the barrel against his leathered leg in a gesture of aimless frustration.

'Go,' he said quietly. Then he shuffled into the darkness of the bedroom, sinking on to the end of the bed.

Colette stared at his back. Why had things come to this? She had loved Mark because he seemed strong, because he made sense of her life. Now, suddenly, it was as if nothing had changed. She had simply exchanged one lost, confused boy for another. Another boy with a gun. Another Danny. She would *not* let it all go to waste.

'You have to take responsibility,' she said.

Mark's head dropped.

'Mark! What's your next move?' He turned to her slowly. *You tell me*, he thought. *For pity's sake, you tell me!*

Christy was stretched out on the living-room sofa when he heard the motorcycle. He lifted his head as it drew closer; when it stopped outside he sprang up, grasping his gun, and eased back the window net.

The bike was parked at the kerb. A figure in leathers and a dark helmet was coming through the gate. About bloody time.

Christy rushed into the hall, quickly positioning himself at the foot of the stairs, shotgun trained on the middle of the front door. As the figure appeared in the frosted glass he fired. The gun barked with a jet of orange flame. The two central panels of the door vanished. Christy glimpsed a body tumbling backwards. He went straight to the door, jerking what remained of it open, and stepped outside.

The motorcyclist lay still on the pathway, visor to the sky, thrown a good yard from the shattered door. Casting a swift glance up and down the street, Christy primed his shotgun again and dropped the barrel to the rider's head. Then, as his finger tightened on the trigger, he paused. A hunk of hair, a good three inches long, showed under the side of the helmet.

Frowning, he bent closer, using the gun barrel to push the visor upwards. It was the face of the strawberry blonde he had seen at D-Day earlier, the pretty one he'd try to chat up. He stood back, stunned.

Across the road a light came on in a front porch. Christy glanced up at it, wiping his mouth. Then, slapping the gun down against his side, he walked briskly through the gate and away down the street.

The sauna was Val's favourite, not one of the largest of the Body Club's private suites, but certainly the most intimate, no more than seven feet by six, barely enough room to lie down. The only light came from the glow of coals in the corner.

His towel draped over his knees, Val sat close to the youth he had picked up, shoulder to shoulder, thigh against thigh. They had talked for nearly twenty minutes, and the sweat was pouring off them.

'So what happened?' Val asked.

The boy shrugged faintly. 'I got sent to a school.' He was growing nervous. He was fresh to this game, but he knew something should have happened by now. He didn't want to talk. He wanted to get back to the quays.

Val reached up, pushing damp hair off the youth's forehead. His eyes were bright. 'What did they do to you?'

The boy blinked, confused. 'Nothing.'

Val's hand closed on his thigh. He leaned closer, his smile brilliant. 'They made you do things . . . .'

'No.' The youth tried to smile back, but something in Val's look stopped him, frightened him; instead he swallowed. The grip on his thigh tightened.

'They did,' Val purred. 'I *know* they did ... .'

The boy shook his head.

'Course they did ... .' Val was nodding, refusing to be denied, locked in some vision of his own. His eyes burned.

The boy's mouth opened in a tiny gasp of pain.

Chapter 26

Mark sat on the floor of the hotel bathroom, jammed between the toilet bowl and the tiled wall, the gun lying in front of him. His face was without colour. His eyes gazed at nothing. In the bedroom a radio murmured softly. Colette stood in the doorway, watching him. Nothing she said, nothing she did seemed to penetrate his blankness. He had gone from her.

'It's Sharon,' she repeated. 'It's on all the stations. The police are looking for you, Mark. They want your help.'

She sank slowly on to her haunches. 'Sharon was warning you!'

It seemed the tone rather than the content of her words that drew his eyes to her; they were dark pools of shadow. 'This is where it all started ... downstairs with Danny ... shooting dope and getting the last bus home.'

Colette sighed, folding her arms over her knees. 'And never growing up,' she murmured.

He gave no sign of hearing her. It was no good. She had tried and tried. She could no longer wait for Mark to act.

Colette rose and slipped quietly from the room, easing shut the door. Sitting on the bed, she turned off the radio and pulled a pocket book from inside her jacket. McGuigan's private number was scribbled on a slip of folded paper attached to the cover with a paperclip. Detaching and unfolding it, she picked up the bedside telephone and dialled for an outside line.

Left alone, Mark allowed his gaze to fall to the shotgun. He reached down and picked it up. One hand took the weight of the barrel, the other caressed the stock. How solid it felt, how compact, how brutally efficient.

What had they called those guns in the old cowboy movies on television? Peacemakers. He wondered if a sawn-off brought anyone any peace. It would be certainly be quicker than a needle. Sharper, cleaner. More dramatic.

He raised the barrel, letting it fall back against his chest, letting the cold, dull metal touch the flesh beneath his jaw. He wondered if Sharon had felt any pain. He hoped not. She'd had troubles enough; she didn't deserve that.

I keep losing people, he thought. *I have a knack for it.* His finger closed on the double trigger.

At first Colette thought that the phone would not be answered. Even McGuigan must go home some time. Was it likely that he would still be at his desk at eleven at night? But she would not ring off. Someone must answer eventually. Someone must know what to do.

The receiver was snatched up.

'McGuigan?' Colette glanced at the bathroom door and spoke in a low murmur. 'This is Colette Adams.'

'Where are you? Are you alright?' The detective sounded breathless, anxious.

The bathroom door opened. Colette started in fear.

Mark appeared, his face still ashen, the shotgun hanging limply by his side. He moved slowly towards her around the bed. Colette relaxed her grip on the receiver, not knowing how to react, not knowing what Mark would do.

He simply nodded at the phone. 'McGuigan?' His voice sounded utterly lifeless.

Colette nodded. She lifted the receiver towards him. He took it and held it limply to his ear. 'Hello, McGuigan.'

'Mark, are you alright? I've been to your house.' His relief was palpable.

'Yeah.' Mark paused. 'How's Sharon?'

'The girl? She's fine – she's going to be alright.' McGuigan spoke quickly, piling information and feeling into his voice, praying the call would last. 'That leather gear you guys wear is something special. She's only concussed.' He stopped, aware of the silence from Mark, afraid he had overdone it.

Mark sank to the carpet, his back against the bed. He could feel relief flooding the upper reaches of his mind – he knew he was pleased for Sharon – but his depression had taken him too deep, to a level where nothing really changed, where he saw things as they really were.

'That was meant to be me,' he said. 'That was supposed to be me.'

'How are you so sure?' McGuigan asked.

'Somebody was in the house when I got back. Christy, I think.'

'Sharon was lucky – you are too, Mark.'

'Danny wasn't lucky, McGuigan. You killed him.'

Colette stared at him. He was talking like someone drugged, like a voice from the grave. Not even Danny had been like this.

'Criminals did, Mark,' said McGuigan firmly. 'Criminals killed him.'

'You knew what you were doing.' An idea floated into Mark's mind. He did not need to think any more. Left alone, the pieces of the puzzle slowly came together on their own. He saw that now. 'But I'm the wild card, aren't I?'

Clutching the receiver, McGuigan frowned. He did not like the way this was going. 'Mark, we can talk this over. We can sort it all out.'

'You do something. They do something back.' Mark nodded faintly. 'It's got its own logic. I can see that.'

'Where are you, Mark?'

It was as if the detective had not spoken. 'Saw you on the

telly a while ago, McGuigan. You were talking about ordinary, decent people needing protection. You're a real Action Man, aren't you, McGuigan? You've got it worked out. Val has too ....'

McGuigan spoke carefully. 'These people aren't everything they're made out to be, Mark.'

Mark sounded tired, tired and lost. 'What are we doing here, McGuigan? Huh? What are we doing with all this Action Man shit?' The plural did not escape the detective.

'Mark,' he asked, 'are you armed?'

'Yeah. From Christy.' Mark let go a slight, ironic chuckle. Then another thought slowly surfaced, and his smile faded. 'They didn't believe the money, no?'

McGuigan sighed. It was all beginning to make sense. Two tip-offs within half an hour. A confused kid trying to put the world to rights, trying to make amends – oh, haven't we all tried the same, Mark?

'I've been around a long time,' he said. 'Just let me know where you are. I'll come over. We'll sort things out. How about that, Mark?'

'We're in a hotel.'

McGuigan nodded, pulling a biro from inside his jacket.

'We're in a hotel ...' Mark's voice seemed to lose all force. There was a long silence. 'Colette'll ring you,' he said suddenly.

The line went dead.

Chapter 27

Colette did not want to rush Mark. She wanted to see him back to normal, or as near as he could manage. She wanted him to put down the shotgun. Stepping round him, she went to use the bathroom. As she closed the door she heard a faint click from the other room. Puzzled, she opened the door again and glanced out. Mark had gone. So had his helmet. So had his gun.

Val straightened his jacket in a long mirror just outside Tony's office, buttoning it carefully across his waist. The pallor had gone from his cheeks; there was warmth in his eyes. God, it was a messy business sometimes, satisfying his appetites. But the relief was a joy that recompensed him for all manner of trouble.

He smiled at himself, savouring the sweet emptiness of repletion. Then he moved a yard or two further down the corridor and ducked into the chief instructor's small office. 'Tony?'

Tony stood beside a filing cabinet, leafing idly through junk mail. He should have closed a good half hour ago, but Val was a favoured customer.

'Give these young fellows a chance,' Val beamed, coming into the room, 'and they turn all queer on you.'

Tony smiled thinly, raising his eyebrows in mock surprise.

Val nodded, pulling his wallet from his back pocket. 'Yeah, neighbour's young fellow. I thought he was going to be alright.' He pulled out a twenty-pound note and handed it to the other man. 'Take care of him, Tony, will you?'

Tony nodded and disappeared in the direction of the sauna. It was a job that was not new to him.

Whistling softly, Val continued down the corridor to the main door. At this late hour the latch was down. As he reached for it, he glanced through the small glass panel set in the door at head height.

There was something wrong with his car. The BMW was parked directly outside, bathed in light from an overhead lamp. Both offside tyres had been slashed to ribbons. Val moved closer to the glass, straining to see beyond the circle of light. Not a sound. No movement in the darkness. Which meant not a thing. Gently he closed the bolt on the door.

It might be kids; it might be someone else muscling in on the smack trade; it might even be that nutter of a biker who'd tried to frame him earlier, though why the hell Christy hadn't crippled him by now was a mystery. Val had not survived this long, achieved this much, by taking chances. Everything about this smelled wrong. He backed away, quickly, down the corridor.

'Tony?' he called softly. 'Tony?'

The chief instructor was in the private sauna suite, splashing cold water on the youth who was now slumped against a corner of the bench, slapping his face repeatedly. He had already slipped the boy's jeans on as high as his crotch; through the open zip, marks of heavy bruising disappeared towards the genitals. The boy moaned, barely conscious.

'Spot of bother outside, Tony,' Val murmured, squeezing into the tiny room. He began tugging at his tie. 'Could do with a small diversion.' He nodded at the youth. 'Come on, dreamboat!'

Mark sat quietly in the darkness of the yard, one boot on the cobbles, another on the bike's footrest. The sawn-off rested between his handlebars, aimed directly at the gym entrance. He had no thoughts, not even of his own luck in tracing Val so quickly. He had only known three places to look, Val's office, D-Day Couriers and here. This had been his second visit.

But he also knew that even this was not luck. He was moving with events now, not attempting to bend them to his own ends. That was the great secret, that was what he had realised talking to McGuigan. Life had a logic of its own. If you fought it, it crushed you, it mangled your brains. If you went with it, you might just stand a chance.

Colette had been right. He had to take responsibility. Responsibility for his emotions, responsibility for his actions. He was still afraid – a part of him quaked in abject terror – but the fear was only a small part of something much bigger now. Something that drove him.

The door to the gym opened. A figure was pushed down the steps below the steel shutter. He looked like a dazed scarecrow, dwarfed by Val's suit jacket, the white collar of his shirt standing up against his neck. From inside Tony's voice called, 'See you, Val!' The door slammed; the outside light winked out.

Mark twisted the ignition key, gunned the engine. His headbeam shot across the yard, transfixing the youth as he stumbled on to the cobbles. Glimpsing Mark's dark helmet, the rising barrel of the gun, the boy shrieked and lurched sideways.

Mark squeezed the trigger. The BMW's nearside windows blew inwards.

Panic-stricken, Val and Tony were suddenly hurling themselves down the entrance steps, leaping for the steel shutter. 'Down!' Val screamed. 'Down!'

Revving the engine, Mark wrenched the throttle, snapped into gear. The bike rocketed across the yard.

The shutter thundered down, so fast it threw Tony off

balance. He slipped, the shutter's edge crashing on to his ankle. At the same instant Mark's bike rammed into it on the other side. Tony bellowed in pain.

Hysterical with rage and fear, Val tried to drag him free. Outside the bike's engine growled as Mark swung round for another run. Tony's foot jerked free. The shutter clunked into its slot.

'Out the back!' Tony yelled, scrambling for the corridor. 'Out the back!'

Val was ahead of him, staring back, eyes blazing. 'Ring the filth!' he bellowed.

Mark crashed into the shutter again, buckling it. The bike twisted under him, engine screaming, throwing him backwards. As it fell on to the cobbles, he sprang up, kicking the shutter, pounding it with his fists, beating at it frenziedly until he was too exhausted to do any more.

Chapter 28

Clad in Tony's windcheater, Val ran to the penthouse flat, only relaxing as the gate slammed on the service lift. He couldn't go home – God knows what the insane bastard had found out about his life by now – but no one knew about his connection with the flat. Only Val, and Christy.

He stumbled into the main room, kicking over decorators' materials, and flicked on the light. Lining paper already covered half the walls. A couple of doors had been painted. He went straight to the furthest, pushing through it into the narrow bathroom beyond. As he rinsed his face in cold water he heard the distant rumble of the retreating lift.

'Shit!' Wiping his face, he reached into the main room and snapped off the light. Then, listening intently, he crossed the room to the main door and positioned himself behind it.

After an age, he heard the lift returning. By the light still filtering from the bathroom he saw a heavy spirit-level lying on the floor. He bent and picked it up.

The lift noise stopped; the gate crashed. Footsteps approached along the corridor. *If it's the courier*, Val thought. *No second chances, no messing about, he's dead.*

A key turned in the lock. Val leaned back, raising the spirit-level. It was a good metre long, wooden and solid.

Christy stepped into the room.

'You stupid fucking bastard!' Val flung the level across the room.

As Christy jerked round in surprise, Val was on him, grasping the front of his jacket, shaking him like a rag doll. 'Why the fuck isn't he *dead*! Why the fuck is he taking pot shots at me! What's he doing with a shooter!'

Forced back across the room, Christy turned from shock to protest to anger. 'He was doing a job for me,' he cried at last.

'For *you*!' Val's face writhed with disbelief, with rage. 'You give some mad dog a shooter? Some *maniac!*'

'Don't blow it, Val!' Christy stared at him; he did not like to be roughed up, especially when he didn't know why; there was violence in his eyes, violence of a controlled kind Val could not match. 'Right?' Christy warned. 'Right?'

Trembling, Val slowly relaxed his grip. It took every effort of self-control to step back. Rage did nothing; rage destroyed. He sucked in breath and turned away abruptly, moving to the window. Suddenly the most intense exhaustion overtook him. Too much had happened today. Too much upset. The whole world seemed to be going mad.

Christy watched him as he sagged against the wall. Whatever had happened, whatever had gone wrong, they had to put things in perspective. They had to be sensible. They were only talking about one kid, for Christ's sake.

'He's not part of anything.' Christy gestured wildly. 'He's an outsider, Val. I've met the guy – he's *nobody*.'

Val sighed and looked down at the lights of the city. For a nobody he was doing bloody well.

Christy's tone changed. He remembered the house. 'He has a chick,' he said suddenly. 'Working in a bank.'

Val's head lifted. 'Do you know her?'

Christy nodded. 'I've seen her a couple of times.'

Val straightened. He took a deep breath, filling his lungs.

Perhaps there was a way out, after all. Perhaps there was hope.

'Good,' he said softly. 'Good.'

John Patrick was tired. The habit of sleepless nights was wearing thin; *that* at least he would happily concede to Dunne. But tonight it had been unavoidable. Two shootings, an attempted murder, an assault on a youth, malicious damage to a house, a gym, a car – and all strongly linked to Val Bourke.

Time was running out for the man. He must realise that. He must know he couldn't wriggle out of it this time. Not unless he reached Mark Wilson before the police did. Not unless Mark reached Val first.

Neither was an outcome McGuigan cared to contemplate. He would have to find them first – find Mark, certainly – even if it meant stopping every motorcyclist in Dublin. It would be a night of waiting, a night of boredom and tension. But he had passed plenty of those before now.

He hoped Mark felt as tired as he did. He hoped his madness would pass and he would find a safe bolthole, sleep the sleep of the exhausted. He did not wish to share a second funeral service with Colette Adams.

He glanced at the wall clock. It was almost two. She should have finished her statement by now. Time she went home. He left Dunne to man the telephones and went downstairs to the interview rooms.

She glanced up as he came in, returning the thinnest of smiles. Her face was wan from tiredness and strain, but she was still pretty, and still strong. Regardless of what she might think of him, McGuigan was impressed by her. She was a sensible girl. She wanted to do what was best for Mark, and she was prepared to face the consequences of that decision. He was a lucky man.

She was reading the statement she had written. 'Fine,' she said quietly, and added her signature. The female officer who had watched her write it nodded to McGuigan as she left.

'We'll arrange a car for you, Colette,' John Patrick said. 'If Mark gets in touch I'd like you to ring me straightaway.'

Colette rose from her chair, her expression serious. 'I think I can be more help than that,' she said.

'Oh, and how's that?'

She looked at him. 'They've seen me leave the bank. Mark told me. They're bound to come for me.'

McGuigan frowned. 'Why?'

'To get at *him*.' She leaned forward, suddenly emphatic. 'I want to be there.'

'No way, love.' John Patrick shook his head abruptly. One member of her family on his conscience was enough.

Colette's face hardened. 'I stood in that toilet, McGuigan.'

'And so did I!' He let her hear his anger. It made no difference.

She folded her arms. 'You put Danny there.'

'OK, OK.' Pricked, McGuigan turned away. She was tougher than he'd thought, more ruthless too. It was another lesson for him. 'You finally said it. And that's what your boyfriend thinks. So now you want me to put you in the firing line as well. I won't do it.'

Colette drew closer to him, her tone softer now, pleading. 'It's a chance, a chance to draw them out . . . .'

Her choice of words stopped his quick answer. Were his own phrases, his own excuses, coming back to haunt him? McGuigan drew in breath, forced to consider what she said. And she was right, of course. If the boy survived the night, Val would be hunting him, Val and Christy. He *was* a wild card. Neither side could predict his next move. To control anything, McGuigan would have to make his own moves. Or suffer the consequences.

He turned back to Colette. 'Where is this bank?' he asked thickly.

Chapter 29

A peremptory tapping at the salon door distracted the girl assistant from her counting, making her lose her place. Annoyed, she glanced up from the cash register.

A motorcyclist stood outside the door. He was dressed in black, his shaded visor down, like the eye of some monstrous insect.

'We don't open till eight thirty,' the girl mouthed, pointing at the opposite wall where a clock registered eight fifteen. She waved her hand back and forth. 'Not open yet.'

The biker tapped again, more urgently.

Scowling now, the girl closed the bag that held the day's float and dropped it into the till, which she closed. It was bad enough being on early turn all week. Alfie got very stroppy about early customers; he was never worth talking to before ten.

Tripping to the door, the girl slipped the lock and opened it a fraction. 'I'm afraid we don't ...'

The motorcyclist pushed past her roughly, rounding on her immediately. He swept his visor up. 'Alfie,' he snapped. His eyes were red-rimmed; his skin greasy and pale.

Frightened, the girl pointed to the back of the shop.

Mark moved briskly away from her, reaching into the front of his jacket.

Alfie yawned and leaned across his desk to switch off the electric kettle bubbling on the far side. Unplugging it, he pulled it closer, pouring scalding liquid into his coffee mug. A portable hi-fi purred Country and Western in the background. The office was a cubbyhole, almost filled by a filing cabinet, the small desk and a plastic swivel chair.

Alfie was barely awake, waiting for the morning's first infusion of caffeine to jar him into activity. The door bursting in on him was a profound shock. Even more was the apparition of Mark, shotgun upraised, pushing him back into his chair.

'Sweet Jes – '

The gun barrel punched into his chest. 'Val!' Mark shouted. 'Where is he?'

Alfie gestured impotently. 'I don't know – Christ – at home . . . .' His face was white.

'He's got no wheels,' Mark snapped. 'He's in the centre – hiding – where!' He cocked the gun.

'Jesus! I don't *know*.' Alfie's eyes grew round with panic. 'Wait – Christy mentioned something – a flat – Abbey Street – on the roof . . . .'

'Number!' Mark shrieked.

Alfie told him.

Mark's hand shot out, snatching the kettle from the desk top. He glanced down at Alfie's chest, his half-buttoned shirt. 'Lot of fuzz there, Alfie,' he hissed, and jerked the kettle forward.

Water jetted from the spout. Alfie started, then screamed as the liquid splashed across his chest. Flinging down the kettle, Mark rushed out.

The operation had been easy enough for McGuigan to organise. Six armed officers: three, including Dunne, in cars parked near the bank entrance, one on the grass to one side – a Browning .38 automatic under his road-sweeper's uniform – another, further back, reading a paper, and the sixth as back-up, sitting next to him in the command car at the end of the roadway. The bank had been alerted, and was co-operating. Staff had been telephoned at home since

156

six thirty this morning, ordered to stay away until further notice.

Speaking to bank officials, McGuigan had mentioned a tip-off about an armed raid just after opening this morning. A very dangerous gang, known to be capable of murder. Only a small white lie, but it concentrated minds wonderfully. If anything went wrong now, the wrath of the National General Bank would be minuscule indeed compared to that of the Garda. McGuigan knew his feet would not touch the ground.

He looked at the dashboard chronometer. Eight twenty-seven. He took a breath and twisted round to Colette in the back seat. 'It's time, love.'

She was gazing out of the window at the bank entrance, her face strained, pale from sleeplessness. She had changed into her work clothes, a short, dark jacket over her white flowing dress.

McGuigan reached out and touched her arm. She started, turning and blinking at him suddenly. He could feel that she was trembling. 'We don't have to do this, you know,' he said softly. 'There's no obligation.'

A toughness he had come to respect rose in her eyes. She steeled herself. 'Yes, there is.'

McGuigan gazed at her steadily a moment, but her look did not waver. He nodded. 'OK. Behave as normally as you can. Go straight to the door – not too fast – not too slow. Ring as you would normally. There's an officer inside. He'll open up on the third ring. If nothing's happened, you'll be taken through the building and out the back. Then, if you're up to it, we might think about another run.'

'I'll be up to it.'

She made him believe it. McGuigan gave her a half smile. *Sweet girl*, he thought. *I wish you were on my side.*

He lifted the walkie-talkie at his side and spoke into it. 'OK, lads, we're on our way.'

Colette opened the car door and climbed out. Immediately she bent to McGuigan's window. 'You know there's only one reason I'm doing this?'

John Patrick nodded, holding her gaze. She moved away.

McGuigan spoke quickly into the walkie-talkie. 'Any hint of trouble – even a suspicion – I want the girl out of it, I want her covered. *No* heroics.'

Colette walked down the cobbles, between the trees. Traffic noise rumbled behind her, but here, surrounded by the architecture of a less frenetic century, its urgency seemed muted, irrelevant. The effect did not add to her sense of reality.

If she had been naked she could not have felt more exposed, more completely vulnerable. She felt like an actress thrust suddenly on stage with no knowledge of the plot she was engaged in, the dialogue, even the character she was meant to portray. She had to force herself to breathe. Ten yards, fifteen, twenty. Not an untoward sound.

She passed the last parked car, glimpsing a fair-haired man sitting stiffly in the front passenger seat. With a jolt she realised he had a sub-machine gun across his lap. *Oh Danny*, she thought. *This is the final debt repaid. If I come out of this we are quits.*

The roadway spread in a broad crescent before the bank entrance. No trees, no parked cars, no cover. She forced herself to cross the bare space, press the bell beside the high, pale wood doors and then step back a few feet, hands clenched, deep in her jacket pockets.

At the far end of the road McGuigan slowly released his breath and thumbed the walkie-talkie. 'Sorry about that lads.'

The sound of a racing engine reached Colette's ears. As she turned her head towards it, a van shot out of nowhere – a large, blue Transit – squealing to a halt between her and

158

the bank entrance. The van's side door was open. Christy, dressed in a boiler suit, hung in the opening. He jumped on to the cobbles, snatching Colette from behind, a heavy automatic pressed over her chest. As he dragged her backwards, she screamed, lashing out with her feet.

The street was suddenly full of running men. Stunned, already hyped up, Christy saw guns everywhere. Dunne was closest, skidding to a halt less than fifteen feet away, legs astride, the black muzzle of his Uzi thrust forward. Gasping, Christy jerked his gun against Colette's throat.

McGuigan tumbled out of his car. 'Don't fire!' he cried into his walkie-talkie, then flung it into the car and ran.

Armed men were snapping into firing position all over the street. But Christy's eyes were on Dunne. The policeman's face was aflame. Christy saw murder in it.

'McGuigan!' he screamed. 'Call them off! Call him off!'

McGuigan appeared through the ring of armed officers, slowing to a walk, raising his arms. 'The girl on the bike!' he called. 'She's OK, Christy – she's OK – just tell us where Val is.'

Dunne sucked in breath audibly. Staring at him, blinking, Christy pressed his gun harder against Colette's neck, making her gasp. 'Call him off, McGuigan!' he roared.

'Tell him!' Colette shrieked. 'Tell him, you bastard!' She kicked suddenly at Christy's shins.

Dunne's Uzi moved another inch forward. Sweat gleamed on his upper lip.

'Dunne, no!' McGuigan gestured fiercely at his sergeant. He came to a halt in the middle of the roadway. His tone changed, became tired, angry, anxious to be done. 'Cut your losses, Christy,' he called. 'Come on – co-operate!'

Christy's eyes flickered from Dunne to the five other faces positioned around the van. Not one wouldn't be delighted at the chance of a crack at him. Not one wouldn't hesitate to shoot. He swallowed. He couldn't take on an army. He wasn't a suicide.

Exhausted, Colette dropped her head against his chest, sobbing quietly. But it was a long minute before Christy opened his arms, pushing her to one side.

'Abbey Street,' he said, and gave the number. His automatic dropped from his hand and clattered on to the cobbles.

No one moved. Colette huddled against the rear of the van, hugging herself. Then McGuigan began walking again, slowly, passing Dunne, reaching the discarded automatic, bending to pick it up off the roadway.

Chapter 30

The address Alfie had given him was a nondescript door beside an office front. There was a single bell push, rusted and unlabelled. Lifting his visor, Mark stepped back to look up at the building. It was a good five storeys, the topmost floor set back and invisible. Frowning, he moved down the pavement. Three buildings, four, five, an unbroken facade.

He went back and tried the opposite direction. Two buildings away was a corner. Turning, he saw what he wanted just one building down. A slim alleyway, guarded by dustbins. He eased round them in deep shadow. Brightness beckoned up ahead.

It was a deep well between close-packed buildings. A funnel of tangled drainpipes, steaming vents, the spidery Meccano of a fire escape climbing to a rectangle of sky. Perfect. .

He crossed the open space and started upward.

Val brushed shaving lather from his cheek and tried to find comfort in his weary reflection. He had hardly closed his eyes all night, not surprisingly since the only overnight accommodation the flat offered had been Christy's discarded sleeping bag. But in the softest bed his mind would not have let him rest.

Without a phone, and unwilling to show his face on the street, he had had to rely on Christy to organise lifting the girl. Given Christy's recent efforts, Val pinned only marginal hopes on his success. If he'd heard nothing by ten, he'd be on his way. The decorators should be in soon. He could borrow overalls. Then a coin-box call to Mary. She'd pack him a bag, bring it down in a taxi. He'd have wheels again by late morning. He could do with a holiday. The businesses didn't need him every day. A few days away. Just until the dust had settled.

The shattering of glass brought him abruptly back to the present, snatched the air from his lungs. Slapping down his towel, Val rushed from the bathroom.

Mark jumped through the gap where the balcony window had been. Seeing Val, he snatched off his helmet, jerked up his gun.

Val stopped dead, his eyes dropping to the barrel. Then the fright went out of him, forced out by a scathing, contemptuous anger. 'I don't know what the fuck you want,' he hissed. 'But whatever it is, you've got it. Right!'

Mark said nothing. His eyes looked glazed, unappreciative of anything.

'OK?' Val snapped. He began backing away, circling towards the middle of the room. The gun barrel followed him. 'You're the one with the gun. You've got it – anything you want ....'

'You're it.' Mark spoke like a sleep walker. 'You're it, Val.' He moved forward.

Val bumped against the decorators' table, stumbled and raised a hand. 'Look, kid, we'd all like to live in a nice, clean world ....'

'But it's not on, Val, is it?' The gun barrel came within inches of his face; Mark was smiling faintly.

Val edged back another step. The guy was a nutter; he had to be mental; he wasn't listening. 'I don't know.' Val shook his head, swallowing. 'Maybe things can be better – maybe we can work something out ....'

'I'm strung out, Val,' Mark said softly.

Val's eyes brightened instantly. Of course he was. That

162

explained the glazed look, the doziness. Everything. 'I can get you turn-ons.'

'I'm strung out on this, Val.' Mark hefted the shotgun in his hands. He sounded almost regretful. 'I've got to do it . . . .'

The panic jumped into Val's throat, almost choking him. 'Now come on, son.' He lifted his hand again. 'I'm warning you . . . .'

'Out!' Mark screamed, his doziness abruptly gone. 'Out on the balcony!' He thrust the gun barrel full into Val's face, his features working in fury. His boot lashed out, sending a chair crashing across the room.

'OK – OK – I'm going.' Shaken, Val turned.

Mark punched him in the small of the back, urging him through the shattered frame of the window, pulling himself up behind him. 'Go on!' Mark punched him again.

Val slithered on the narrow steps outside. 'Please – ' he snapped. 'Don't push me – don't push . . .'

'Go *on!*' Mark bellowed.

Val touched the iron grid of the balcony. He clutched at the railing, holding tight as he saw the drop to the well.

Mark squeezed beside him, gun upraised. 'How's the view, Val?' His teeth were bared in a grin of hatred; he seemed possessed. Panting, Val twisted, sinking into the corner of the balcony.

'Are you frightened?' Mark shouted. '*Are* you?' His grin vanished. 'Climb!'

The gun was pointed at Val's throat. Val stared over it into the boy's eyes. He saw hatred in them, he saw fear, but, he realised suddenly, no relish for violence, no need for it. Something else had driven him to this. Christy was right. The kid was a dummy, a nobody.

'No,' Val said softly. His lip curled in contempt. 'You haven't the bottle, have you?' His hand snatched at the gun, gripping the barrel. Rising, he forced it downward,

163

struggling against Mark. 'Pull the trigger, you bastard!' he hissed. 'Pull the fucking trigger – *pull* it!' He spat in Mark's face.

The gun barked. The shot ripped into Mark's leg, shredding the leather, splaying blood across the ironwork. Grunting in pain, Mark fell back against the railing.

Val jerked the gun from his hands. Breathing heavily, he grasped Mark's leather jacket, pushing him back over the iron rail, jamming the gun barrel under his chin. He was shaking violently from reaction, barely able, in his mounting rage, to form the words. 'Why did *you* have to stick your face in? Who the *fuck* do you think you are? You little bastard – *why*!'

The gun forced Mark's head further and further back over the drop. He could not swallow; he could hardly breathe. His blood pumped through the balcony grating. Val was screaming, foam flecking his lips. 'You should have known better than to fuck with me!'

A movement came from one side. 'Val!' a voice called.

Blinking, Val jerked his head round. McGuigan stood in the archway leading to the flat roof. Val pushed Mark aside, swivelled the shotgun.

John Patrick raised his hand, staring down the barrel. 'Just calm yourself, Val,' he said.

Val sucked in breath, his mouth twisting in a savage grin. 'How's it going, McGuigan?' he cried. 'Just in fucking time, as usual!' He lifted the gun higher, taking aim.

'Two cartridges, Val,' Mark said suddenly from the floor. Wild-eyed, Val glanced down at him. An eery grin fixed Mark's features. His eyes rose to the roof above Val's head.

Frowning, Val spun, lifting his head. Dunne stood just above him, glaring down the barrel of his Uzi.

'Val!' McGuigan shouted.

Dunne fired, emptying his magazine in a concussive burst. Bloody pits erupted across Val's chest. The force of their impact pitched him backwards. He struck the railing and jack-knifed over the top.

Mark lurched forward to the balcony edge. He saw Val turning over as he fell, a slow, graceful, unreal somersault in empty air. Then, with a soft thud, he was a broken doll on the concrete floor of the well, daubed with poster-paint red, spreadeagled like a Manx figure. Like a ripe fruit dashed on to hard ground. Except that, like Danny, he was dead.

Chapter 31

In Mark's dreams Val fell perpetually, carving lazy circles in the sky. In his nightmares Val was a broken body smeared on concrete, a bloody human caricature, who sprang suddenly upright, dead eyes blazing, lips white with foam. 'Why do *you* have to stick your face in! Who the *fuck* do you think you are!' While Dunne's Uzi rattled in the background, on and on and on . . . .

Mark jerked awake, snapping his head off the pillow. Heart churning, he stared across the darkened bedroom, not knowing where he was, or who. Slowly, calm returned, and the rattling sound became recognisable. It came from downstairs, someone playing with the new front door knocker. Daylight showed through from the landing. The bedroom curtains were still pulled. Mark's digital alarm read nine thirty.

He threw back the duvet, reached out for the crutches propped next to his bed and hauled himself upright. The pain still bit, but the doctors had told him that the shattered tendon was knitting well. It was to be expected. He hobbled out on to the landing and, with some difficulty, descended the stairs.

The young couple outside were turning away as he cracked open the door. 'Oh,' the girl smiled; she was dark and straight-haired, faintly prim-looking. 'We've come about the house . . . .' Her eyes dropped to Mark's underpants, his only piece of clothing, and her face fell. 'Oh . . . .' 'We can call back,' the man said quickly.

'No.' Mark smiled, pulling the door wide open. 'No,

come in. Look around.' He moved back to allow them past. Awkwardly the girl stepped forward.

'Take your time,' said Mark, closing the door. 'I'll be in here.' He hobbled after them, knocking open the kitchen door with a crutch. Inside he filled a kettle, switched it on and began spooning tea into a pot. He was leaning against the sink unit, sipping from a mug when the couple re-appeared.

They paused in the middle of the floor, looking about at the wall cupboards, the table, the dresser and, finally, Mark. The girl had still not overcome her embarrassment. 'How much are you looking for?' she asked.

Mark turned to them, gazing over his tea. 'How much have you got?'

The girl glanced nervously at the young man. He wore a business shirt and a tie; he looked very serious. 'Well, I suppose we could stretch to ...' He shrugged. 'Let's see, about ...'

'Fine,' said Mark.

'Pardon?' the young man said.

Mark shrugged easily. He smiled. 'Fine. Whatever you can stretch to.' Surprised delight transformed the girl's face. She put her hand to her mouth.

'Are you serious?' the young man asked.

'Yeah,' Mark said simply. His smile spread. The couple stared at each other, not knowing how to react. Untroubled, Mark drained his mug. Selling houses was easy. He should have done it years ago.

It was a warm day for late October, the sun bright, the sea smooth across Dublin Bay. From the height of the Bull Wall, Mark and Colette watched the old men splash like two-year-olds in the water below the concrete bathing shelters.

It had been Mark's longest walk since giving up his

crutches, a good mile out into the water. Colette had brought him in her father's car. Mark was wheel-less now, his Suzuki sold weeks ago. He wouldn't have been able to ride it for months, and he'd needed the money. His helmet and leathers had gone too. He didn't mind. Not seriously.

Healing, he'd learned, was about moving on, about opening up to new things, new experiences. In the house in Marino he had been locked up in the past, locked up in his own head, trying to make broken pieces fit.

An engine whined behind them. Colette turned and waved suddenly, jogging his elbow. Mark looked round, and grinned.

A large motorcycle purred along the causeway and jolted to a halt beside them. Sharon pulled off her helmet and beamed at them. She had on a new leather suit in bright pink. Across her front she wore an even newer courier vest - red fluorescent letters against a spotless white background: Mayday Couriers. The telephone number had once belonged to D-Day. She swivelled to show an identical message on her back. 'What do you think?' she grinned.

Mark laughed. 'It's magic. Congratulations.' The irony of it pleased him. With Carol gone, it had only needed someone to pick up the pieces. Courier companies should be run by people who knew the job.

'I'm really glad for you, Sharon,' Colette smiled.

Sharon nodded. 'How about you?' she asked.

Mark shrugged, glancing with a smile at Colette before replying, 'I don't know.'

'We're thinking of leaving,' Colette said.

'For good?'

'Maybe,' said Mark.

Sharon's smile reasserted itself. She had once thought that she and Mark might have got together. There had been opportunities, but it had been Colette who had prised open his armour. They had become an item, she could see that.

169

They even behaved like a couple. Sharon didn't mind, not now. 'No more messing, eh?' Her look was momentarily coquettish.

Mark had the grace to blush. 'I'll give you a ring,' he promised her.

She glanced down at her vest. 'You know where I am.'

'See you, Sharon,' Colette grinned.

Sharon took her cue. She pulled on her helmet, pressed the electric starter and purred away. They watched her go then, exchanging smiles, turned and walked slowly on.

'I still can't believe I nearly killed her,' said Mark after a pause.

Colette looked at him: his eyes followed the ground. 'You were somebody else out there,' she said quietly.

'I know . . . .' He thought of Val, he thought of McGuigan, he thought of a bike smashing impotently against a steel shutter, screams in the night, days of madness. He thought of Danny.

Then he looked up and saw the crease of anxiety in Colette's forehead. And – with an effort that grew easier with every passing day – forgot.

His arm reached out, snaking round her waist. 'So,' he said, 'what do you think?'

Colette turned to him; her face lightened. 'About leaving?'

'Yeah.' He was quite positive.

Her smile broadened. Leaning close, she hooked an arm over his shoulder, drawing him towards her until their noses touched.

'I think we should stick together,' she told him.